D1095392

Helping Verbs of the Heart

Helping Verbs of the Heart

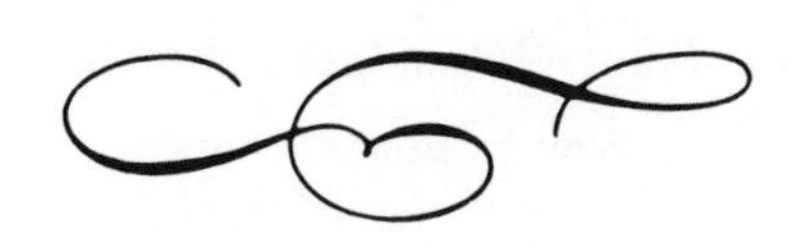

PÉTER ESTERHÁZY

Translated from the Hungarian by
Michael Henry Heim

GROVE WEIDENFELD
New York

Published by Grove Weidenfeld
A division of Grove Press, Inc.
841 Broadway
New York, NY 10003-4793

Published in Canada by General Publishing Company, Ltd.

Originally published in Hungarian as *A szív segédigéi* by Magvető, 1985

Library of Congress Cataloging-in-Publication Data

Péter Esterházy, 1950–
[Szív segédigéi. English]
Helping verbs of the heart / Péter Esterházy ; translated from the Hungarian by Michael Henry Heim.—1st American ed.
p. cm.
Translation of: A szív segédigéi.
ISBN 0-8021-1123-8
I. Title.
PH3241.E85S9613 1991
894′.51133—dc20 90-36220
CIP

Manufactured in the United States of America

Printed on acid-free paper

Designed by Irving Perkins Associates

First Edition 1991

1 3 5 7 9 10 8 6 4 2

Foreword

He who can hope can speak, and vice versa.
LUDWIG WITTGENSTEIN

The stories people write nowadays are all very beautiful, meaningful, deep and useful, full of temperament or serenity. Only they have no introduction. That is why I've decided to write this story in such a way as to require an introduction.

It's nearly two weeks since my mother died, and I'd better get to work before the urge I felt so violently during the funeral, the urge to write about her, turns back into the lethargic wordlessness I felt at the news of her death.

Yes, to work! Because while the need to write about my mother still comes on me unexpectedly, it can be very vague, that is, I must stop myself from giving in to the whim of the moment and thwacking a single key till it covers the paper: m m m m m mmm m mmmmmmmm m mmm m m m

I don't use language, I don't wish to discover the truth, even less to lay it before anyone. Nor would I dream of naming the world, as a result of which I don't name a thing in the world: naming is tantamount to making a permanent sacrifice of name to named. . . .

I don't speak, but I'm not silent, which isn't the same. I'm cautious: this is about my mother. Maybe the whole thing should go into italics. No, damn all prostitutalics! Why is it more perverse to write about her than to say nothing? *Or anything else!* Standing by the grave! What in the world is that supposed to mean?! Or taking her hand and waiting for her to squeeze! Watching the cells go out into the world: *au revoir, monsewer,* think of us as part of your mother; bye-bye, you silly little, pretty little boy! mmmm m m A grown man lays not his grief before the world.

I'm terrified, yet I feel better now: time passing doesn't hurt.

The worst thing that could happen at this point is a show of sympathy—a look, a word even. I'd turn away or hush the speaker, because what I need to feel is that the things I'm going through can be neither understood nor shared; it's the only way I can believe there's some sense and truth to the horror of it all. The moment it turns into words, I am overcome with ennui and the whole thing seems pointless again. Now and then I do mention Mother's death to this or that person, but it makes no sense and I'm furious if they dare to comment. I'd rather they distracted me, teased me about something.

In his last film James Bond tosses the enemy over a railing, and when asked whether the man is *dead* he says, "I should hope so!" Well, I laughed a relieved laugh. Jokes about death and the dying don't bother me at all; I even enjoy them.

Yet there were times when I lost my head and suddenly everyday concepts, *basic* concepts I had reeled off for years, decades, came undone, and my consciousness throbbed, and a void came to fill it. . . . Now that's over; I don't lose my head anymore. When I write, I necessarily write about the past, about things I've put behind me—at least by the time I write about them. No matter what a book is about, it should radiate a kind of lightness, a reminder that a work of art is never something given, taken for granted, but rather a combination of *demand* and *gift*.

I make literature, as usual, by defamiliarizing and objectifying reality into a memory-and-formulation machine. The world exists to be turned into a book, says Mallarmé. I'm not even ashamed of it; I've become resigned to having the face that my books display. But now I'm going to change that.

The text includes quotations, either literal or distorted, from, among others, Miklós Apáti, H. C. Artmann, Mihály Babits, Donald Barthelme, Georges Bataille, Thomas Bernhard, Jorge Luis Borges, Albert Camus, Anton Chekhov, Jenő Dsida, Péter Esterházy, Milán Füst, Péter Hajnóczy, Peter Handke, Gyula Illyés, Vsevolod Ivanov, István Jelenits, Ferenc Juhász, Valentin Kataev, István Kormos, Dezső Kosztolányi, Lautréamont, Stéphane Mallarmé, Iván Mándy, Miklós Mészöly, Ferenc Molnár, Robert Musil, Ottó Orbán, Géza Ottlik, Blaise Pascal, Saint Paul, János Pilinszky, Arthur Rimbaud, Jean-Paul Sartre, Ronald Sukenick, Lőrinc Szabó, Lev Tolstoy, Georg Trakl, Szabolcs Várady, István Vas, Péter Vasadi, Sándor Weöres, and Ludwig Wittgenstein.

What a spinster I must be! I'm not brave enough to love death.

Given at Buda, on this the 16th of June

In the name of the Father and the Son—

We had known for years that Mother "was feeling generally rotten," yet when Father phoned and informed us with grave concern and in a stern voice we'd never heard before that Mother was thus and so and he thought—it was his personal conviction—that "at a time like this" we might *be at home,* that is, come home, it took us by surprise, and we each started hemming and hawing in nearly identical terms, pleading the exigencies of the daily grind, which didn't mean we were indifferent or insensitive, no, it was just a natural impulse, the sober conviction that "whatever it was" couldn't be "all that dangerous," because it never had been before (and as Father himself was wont to say, "Trouble doesn't start till there's trouble, but the moment there's trouble it starts"). When Father snarled back at us, though, we flocked home from the four corners of the earth.

IT'S COLD. . . . WHEN WE PUT OUR CLOTHES ON, SHE WAS VERY SURPRISED TO SEE ME IN A BLACK TIE, AND SHE ASKED ME IF I WAS IN MOURNING. I TOLD HER MY MOTHER HAD DIED. SHE ASKED WHEN, SO I ANSWERED, "YESTERDAY." SHE RECOILED SLIGHTLY BUT SAID NOTHING. I FELT LIKE TELLING HER IT WASN'T MY FAULT, BUT I HELD BACK BECAUSE I REALIZED I'D SAID IT TO MY BOSS. IT DIDN'T MEAN A THING. BESIDES, A PERSON IS ALWAYS SOMEWHAT AT FAULT.

As if by secret agreement with Mother I got to the hospital before my brother and sister. Not that she loved me best; no, she loved my brother more, though maybe *only* because she knew he needed her most and loved her most intensely in exchange. I'm the firstborn; I *had* to arrive first. . . . By definition.

My sister is the best-looking of us, I think; she has Father's fragility and Mother's fire. Women prefer my brother, but my women prefer me. The only trouble is I'm too personal: I am [corrupt text] tailored to the individual. True, it makes no difference in the end.

My sister immediately threw her arms around me—"What do you say, old buddy, old boy!"—and squeezed me long and hard. Her abandon wasn't unexpected, it brought back thousands of memories, and I gave in to it reluctantly; I didn't like her being so well acquainted with the power of body contact that she could use it practically like a pro, without thinking, and I felt that she was abusing it and went on stroking me when a pat on the back would have done the trick, that she was making overly sure of me, and that it was more style than something genuinely personal on her part. I didn't feel that it meant much to her, only that she knew it did to me. Which was true.

In the end, of course, it was a fitting gesture, because it achieved its goal, and I melted as I held that beautiful, slender blond in my arms, I rejoiced in her fragrance and her ribs, her impossible, careless makeup, the arch of her mouth reminiscent of my brother's, the closeness of her face, the many familiar curves, each of which might have been one of mine—the convoluted property relations

made me first furious and impatient, then docile, moved—I rejoiced in her voice repeating with sarcasm and respect, "Well, well, old buddy! At last, old boy!"

YOU'VE GOBBLED UP YOUR MOTHERS! (I'VE GOBBLED UP MY MOTHER.)

The remaining sibling cleared his throat in the background like a husband caught in the act, then pushed us apart with exaggerated gestures and a "Who is this man, you tart!?" and so on, grim and ridiculous. The hospital visitors turned to look as they hurried by.

We forgot why we'd come and just stood there making fools of ourselves. But when we went through the large, rusty iron gate—like everyone who goes through the large, rusty iron gate—we quieted down, though we kept up a self-assured flutter that was out of keeping with our age, like people on their way to a gala *tea* where they will be the center of attention, which they will tolerate with aplomb, trampling hearts without mercy, the brothers threatening their sister's suitors, while she goes on arousing them until the latter up and give the former what for, and if at first, tittering in complicity, they merely retire to a corner, behind a screen, to far-off rooms, after a while they go dancing round and round, through the rooms, laughing feverishly, and the former join in, though . . . though they hadn't the slightest desire to, really.

On the border of orphanhood and self-deception, or essentially beyond it, a sadder and frailer trust would have been more suitable.

When we got to the gatehouse, my brother leaned over to the window and with his usual breezy flair ordered the bewildered old gatekeeper to give him his wrist. Then grabbing it and making a series of self-important grimaces, he said solicitously, "Very high, old man, and that's not low. You must be very, very careful." Whereupon he gave us a wave and said, "Time to go, colleagues," and in we went. We were bursting with laughter when the silence suddenly broke in on us. And

God smote our hearts with His rough finger. We stopped short. From then on we couldn't look one another in the eye: whoever did—and we did over and over—burst into helpless tears. That was ridiculous too. All we needed to say was "Burst!"

LEST HE BE RECOGNIZED, THE ARCHANGEL ASSUMED THE FORM OF A VICUÑA-SIZED PURSE CRAB. "YOU HAVE DONE A FINE, ANEMIC JOB OF CAPTURING DEATH. YOUR PANGS OF CONSCIENCE WERE SIMPLY FANTASTIC."

The nurse led us down the dimly lit corridor in silence. The first thing I thought when I saw her (I couldn't stop myself, though I tried) was that she was evil, evil to the core, the malicious kind, who not only embodied evil but caused it, perhaps even carried in bacteria, and with a fat profit in mind; one thing was dead certain, though: it was her job to do away with problem patients.

In the distance, waiting for us at the entrance to the shapeless side wing, she had seemed thin, a thin, severe, nunlike figure flat against the wall, but as we drew closer, we could see she had simply laced herself up tightly—with her dress, her apron straps, anything and everything—and that too I held against her: the furtiveness of it all made her full, curvaceous hips repulsive, and not even the delicate blond curls hiding demurely beneath her cap could alter my impression. We glared at each other with hatred in our eyes, her snub nose and thick, glistening lips revealing first stupidity, then sensuality (as if one excluded the other).

AT LAST HE CRIED OUT, "MAN, WHEN YOU SEE A DEAD DOG TRAPPED IN A SLUICE, DON'T DO WHAT OTHERS DO, DON'T SCOOP OUT THE MAGGOTS BREEDING IN ITS BLOATED BELLY, DON'T WATCH THEM IN AMAZEMENT, DON'T FLICK OPEN YOUR JACKKNIFE AND SLASH THE MAGGOTY MASS TO BITS AT THE THOUGHT THAT YOU MAY BE NEXT! WHAT SECRET ARE YOU AFTER? NEITHER I NOR THE ARCTIC POLAR BEAR'S FOUR WEBBED PAWS HAVE SOLVED THE MYSTERY OF LIFE. BEWARE! NIGHT IS APPROACHING AND YOU'VE BEEN HERE SINCE MORNING. WHAT WILL YOUR FAMILY AND YOUR LITTLE SISTER SAY IF YOU COME HOME LATE? WASH YOUR HANDS AND TAKE THE ROAD LEADING TO YOUR BED. . . ."

In one of the beds an old man, his haggard face overgrown with white stubble, was gesticulating madly, screaming at a thin nurse. "Don't you touch me! . . . Only a signorina can touch me!" The girl shrugged. "I won't let you!" "Tell her you're Italian," my brother whispered to her. "I'm Italian, sir." The old man's face lit up for a moment, then he turned to the nurse and us with a look that said he was on to everything, including that we took him for a fool, and shouted, "The signorina's no Italian; the signorina's lying. If the signorina were Italian, she'd be hot and I'd feel it. But the signorina's slimy, cold as a toad. Mark my words, the signorina is a Central European, a normal whatsit. She's got as much in common with life as . . . as I have!" The girl burst out crying; her yellow hair fell limply into a tearstained face. Even as we moved on, we could see the old man flailing his arms and deliriously tearing out catheters and IV- and blood-transfusion tubes. "As much in common! As much in common!" he kept repeating.

The nurse pointed to a corner with the indifference of a checkout girl:

"That's your mother."

My brother, who had stood stiffly till then, gave a frightened shake of the head and lunged forward. The nurse slipped past us with an almost friendly "What's so terrible?," her heavy breasts (they were a burden slung round her neck; she seemed to sag under their weight) brushing against my arm. I saw that my sister saw, and I could tell what she thought. I started thinking about myself in self-defense.

The person she had pointed to, our mother, had a gray face and a nose stuffed with absorbent cotton, clearly to stop the bleeding. *Everything was wrong.* Even the colors seemed off-center, oblique. We looked around almost simultaneously and noted something much more alarming: she in no way differed from her roommates. Though we'd have been hard put to say what they were, those curious, remote objects with tubes coming out of them in complex configurations and wind whistling through their sunken lips. Mother too wheezed air in like a machine—our only indication she was alive. There was nothing for us to recognize.

GREKOVA: WHERE DOES IT HURT?
PLATONOV: PLATONOV HURTS ALL OVER.

"It's the end," my sister declared. The improbability, the incredibility of the moment, she said later outside the hospital, had given her the frivolous idea that if what is were not, then anything would be possible; she felt like an empty hole, she said, a dark rift gouged into the air. I could think of nothing except that my helplessness was a *mistake* that should not have been allowed to happen.

My sister had unerringly identified the only familiar detail, and delicately leaned down to Mother's hand. Once more her delicacy filled me with disgust; she could do nothing right that day, the poor dear. "Let us pray," I said, by which I meant pray and get going. My brother spun round to me with burning eyes, as if he'd been bitten by a treacherous papist viper and I'd made a wise-crack or said a dirty word. Not daring to calm him down, I launched into the Lord's Prayer like a black marketeer. My sister made a face, because since childhood we'd thought of Our Father as our father, our very own, or, rather, we'd tried to shoo the thought away, which shooing process we called "saying the Lord's Prayer."

MOTHER'S FINGERS SET OFF IN FORMATION AND MERGED ON A THIN BONE-FURROWED SURFACE. THE PART THAT WOULD COME INTO CONTACT WITH OUR FACES WHEN SHE SLAPPED US, THE VEINS ON THE BACK OF HER HAND, HAD TURNED INTO A TERRIFYING MAP. LIVER SPOTS AND RED OR EVEN PURPLE PATCHES MADE THE MAP IMAGE MORE PLAUSIBLE. THE SKIN WAS LIKE A GLOVE THAT DID NOT QUITE FIT. A SMALL PIECE OF FLESH HAD SLIPPED DOWN TO THE BASE OF THE THUMB, AND THE PALM WAS SHINIER THERE. THE ABOVE-MENTIONED GLOVE WAS

FINELY CRAFTED, DELICATE AND SILKY, THOUGH CHAPPING HAD (HERE AND THERE) AGGRAVATED THE WRINKLES.

FATHER'S FACE WAS COVERED WITH UGLY CUTS, HIS FEATURES SCREWED INTO WHAT LOOKED LIKE A BADLY WOUND BALL OF TWINE, BUT THOSE FINGERS, EVEN WHEN THEY RAPPED AGAINST HIS CHEEKBONE, SET OUT WITH A PROMISE OF REDEMPTION. FATHER, SENSING PERHAPS THE TERRIFYING HALF-MOONS ON THOSE NAILS OF HOPE, GAVE A SUDDEN SNORT, AND ONLY THEN WAS IT CLEAR HOW REPULSIVE THAT BALL OF TWINE REALLY WAS. MOTHER'S HAND WITHDREW IN AN ARC (LIKE A QUESTION MARK, THICK AND CATEGORICAL).

Mother's doctor watched us from the door. We couldn't tell a thing from his face. He was a friend of my brother's. "Your mother, she's got death in her innards." That's what he said. I didn't like his tone. A man shouldn't side with death, put himself on a par with it. Even if he's a doctor—in other words, even if he knows a trick or two, if he sometimes sees the emperor has no clothes. "Your mother might hurry her death along," he said, nodding, and when I glared at him, he added theatrically, "No need to be shocked. I'm a Voltairian." "I see," I nodded back, offended. "Neither death nor its master, God, takes us seriously. There is only one response worthy of man. Not to take them seriously." I was afraid of him. When I looked at him, which I tried desperately not to do, I felt I'd known him for a thousand years, and I had a disagreeable thought: Death is something you have to want.

On the way out a pale, moist hand extended from one of the beds—a hostile creature, a pernicious growth—and clasped my sister. Frightened and repelled, I stared at the pale arm. An old woman had sat up in the bed and was screaming at my sister as if she knew who she was. "You!" My sister, annoyed, tried to tug her hand free, but the woman squeezed it with monstrous strength. Her hand stiffened convulsively; horrendous; all mothers have the same hands! "You killed me, *you shadow,* you killed me in '56!" "Let her have her way," someone whispered quickly. "Yes, I did." "Shadow," she said, "shadow's not the half of it! Admit it! You never loved me! The only reason you needed me was—" "That will do!" I shouted like a schoolmaster, and ran out. Then: "Why did you admit

it?" I asked. "Are you crazy?" my sister said, staring at me as if I were an utter stranger.

"WE THOUGHT LIFE WAS A FEAST AND SOMETHING WAS AWAITING US."

Outside we made believe we had things to take care of. We had nothing to say to one another, nothing to say to anyone, nothing to think. And we had no time to ease our condition with confessions or professions, to admit that we weren't up to our own grief or affected by the insolence of sur-vival or that none of it hurt quite enough; it was all but intolerable, our dwarflike nature, which left the *what's-its-name* meaningless. Because life depends on forms, and of forms there are fewer and fewer. Left to our own devices, we wallow in our own dirt. Shit, how annoying.

It was putrefyingly hot in front of the hospital, a pernicious August heat, a putrid summer, everything peeling, coming apart, coming apart, our soles smacking against the asphalt, putrid air . . . Everything stinks of shit—don't try to deny it!—the stench streaming out of white rooms, trams, churches, relatives, out of us; humidity oozing out of cracks; passersby dragging spewed-out strips of gauze; yellow stains on men's trousers; and flies, flies, wherever you look! Sweltering heat and the stench of shit. A putrid summer! Eating yourself up, damn your rotten soul . . . !

DAMNED GOD-PIGS! AND THE CHRIST-GNOME WHO IS NOT, TAP-DANCING IN PATENT LEATHER SHOES ON THE STAGE THAT IS THIS WORLD, SITTING ON THE THRONE WHERE THE CHIEF MAGISTRATE SITS, NO HEAVEN ABOVE, SWOLLEN HANDS ATREMBLE, GLASSY-EYED AND BELCHING, LOOKING DOWN ON US, ON US HIS PEOPLE, WHO JUST KEEP CHUMUNCHING AWAY. MMMM M MM M MMM

I woke up early on the day of the funeral (a hard day's day), excited as if going on a trip or the stage. Already I'm a guest in the parental house. Father surmised from the noise that I was up but not that I might like to be alone a *little* longer, and he came right in. He was pleasant and accommodating, a kind of elder brother, which is what he's generally like unless his interests dictate otherwise. We discussed the order of bath and breakfast in our usual roundabout way, which we always enjoyed more than we expected. *"You're a real mother to me, Dad,"* I said, but he only smiled. He said he'd make bacon and eggs and run my bath. I'll never have his flair. As a child I'd try to "outguess the bacon," predict the moment it would turn glassy. Bacon and eggs was a treat in those days; in other words, we must have been quite poor or, rather, living in poverty.

I sat down to breakfast in my brother's huge and memorably soft pajamas—foreign pajamas! a man's nightshirt! Meanwhile my sister arrived—we were gathering like a herd—and somewhat rearranged the morning's activities; she mothered us, a morning flimflam I have a hard time forgiving her. The table was laden with a wicker basket of soft-boiled eggs and plates of salmon, cold roast beef, clams, Transylvanian and boiled bacon, tomatoes, peppers, various kinds of bread and toast. I made the simple, resolute, and pedantic suggestion—a sort of itinerary for the rest of the summer holidays—that *when the time came* we should refrain from crying. "I've got some tranquilizers here," I said. My sister gave me a frightened glance, my brother went on eating in his customarily immod-

erate manner, and our father made a face that said, "A man doesn't talk like that."

BY THAT DAY THE MOTHERS HAD GROWN EXTREMELY HEAVY WITH THEIR ROCKABYES, THEIR BELLIES DARK AND DOWNY, SHINY AND TIGHT, THEIR BREASTS ALL BUT ENORMOUS AND COMICALLY MISMATCHED, THE NIPPLES AND THEIR COURTYARDS ROUGH AND A BRAND-NEW BROWN, EVERY TINY PIECE OF THEM ALIVE, HEAVY AND ALIVE, HEAVY AND ALIVE. . . .

While I was in the bath, my father and brother, sitting on the wastepaper basket or leaning against the door, argued about how to deal with condolences after the funeral. My brother refused to participate under any circumstances, he said; he was no clown, he said, and he didn't give a damn about the others, they could let him have that luxury, it was *his* mother who'd died, after all. "And mine."

Father made some subdued, unobtrusive references to tradition, then gave a less subdued but by no means emotional lecture on tact, egotism, and the like. He spoke in a manner befitting a paterfamilias, not particularly wishing to convince us apparently: this and that was thus and so. Which I found offensive in principle, and I called his attention to the weak points in his "arguments," for instance, to the fact that convention would be satisfied if he alone accepted condolences at the graveside and that if we did remain with him it would only be out of love and respect (it was the first time in my life I had told my father, even in so roundabout a fashion, that I loved him), in other words, carefully weighing our own interests and his wishes he might be expected at least to sense the conflict, the obedience conflict. No, Father said, he saw no conflict worthy of the name, and he looked around like a six-year-old, all innocence and impatience. He was (justifiably) biased against my brother for skirting the issue, looking for a chance to disagree, *shooting off his mouth,* and being pubescently proud of it, and he called me needlessly *precious,* all words and no show, a real temporizer, though my point of view tallied with his. "It does not."

WHERE THERE IS TYRANNY, THERE IS TYRANNY: OUR FATHER IS ERGO OUR FATHER: A EST A.

At that point, at that momentous and dignified point in time, Father, as in one of those wonderful Czech films of the sixties, gave his trousers an unexpected and violent tug and stood there in his drawers, informing us he was off to the throne of the house for some big business that would brook no delay, during which of course our exceedingly barren—if important in principle—*pourparlers* could piddle along. . . . Clearly Father was not joking, and when he began waddling trouser-hobbled in the direction of the toilet I jumped out of the bath, draped myself in a giant, warm, soft, fluffy bath towel dating back to our grandmother, and marched off, haughty and indignant, after my brother. Outside the door we could hear him laughing, laughing at us, his fastidious progeny, laughing a laugh indistinguishable from tears.

I gave myself a good spray. Only now did I realize what a dangerous day it was. If the day of the funeral were only the funeral, there would still be a chance, and no one could possibly lift an arm and glance back under his arm in a cloud of scent bemoaning his helplessness, his dreadful loneliness, other people's heartlessness, God's mercilessness, God's nonexistence. *Words are all too tame.* Father remarked that my tie was not solid black, and I let it register without responding; it was so obvious—who but Father could have made a point of it? He ordered, I obeyed. I bought an awful solid black one at the local tobacconist's (!) and tried several times to deposit it in one of the cemetery litter baskets, but each time I had the feeling that then, just then, at that very moment it was impossible. I've

been to several funerals with it since, the latest being Illyés's.

FANCSIKÓ POUNCED ON FATHER WITH A FORCE THAT BELIED HER CONTEMPLATIVE EXPRESSION. "POW! POW!" THE LEATHER SLIPPER EXPLODED IN HIS FACE. MY FATHER LOOKED UP FROM BETWEEN HIS BROKEN SHOULDERS. "WHY?" HE PROTESTED SOFTLY. I SQUATTED, COWERING ON THE BLOCK OF MY TRUTHS.

By the time we were ready to leave, my father and my brother stood glaring at each other; it was too late to separate them. Though how good it would have been if what happened hadn't. And of course I'm the one who remembers everything. "What are you saying! You're the one! You're the one who murdered Mother! You!" Father's eyes narrowed to slits, as if he were looking at a far-off object, his son, and full of suspicion and hate he shouted to his face, "What do you know about my life, boy?" "Come off it, will you! All you do is pity yourself. Why, you're playacting this very minute." Father took off his glasses—his face was suddenly alien—and began to clean them, using the corner of his jacket as he might a sweater.

OUR BROTHER IS DEAD: COLD HIS FEET, COLD HIS BELLY, COLD HIS CHEEKS, COLD HIS HEART, COLD THE WOUND ON HIS BREAST MADE BY OUR IRON. NO ONE CAN RISE AGAINST US NOW. YOU ARE THE KING OF KISS, OUR BROTHER LAUGHS FROM BENEATH THE EARTH. HE COULD HAVE BEEN A MIGHTIER LORD THAN WE, MIGHTIER AND BRAVER. HIS GREATNESS CAN BE MEASURED ONLY BY HIS MISERY. OUR BROTHER WAS EMPTY; WHAT HE TOUCHED BECAME EMPTY. HE NEVER DENIED BEING PLUNDERED, OR AT LEAST RARELY, WHICH IS WHY WE LOVED HIM SO. AND IF WE HATED HIM, IT WAS ONLY BECAUSE WE ENVIED HIM. NOW WE WOULD BE GLAD TO LOOK HIM IN THE FACE: OUR PRIDE IS WORTHY OF IT. HIS FACE WAS A BROWNISH YELLOW, AT ONCE CREOLE AND PALE. (MY GOOD MOTHER USED TO SAY, "THAT COLOR—THAT'S WHAT THE WOMEN GO FOR.") OUR

BROTHER'S BURNED HIMSELF OUT, IS WHAT WE SAID IN COMPANY.

IT IS COLD NOW. TIME THE MISER IS SHRINKING. A WIND ARISES FROM AMONGST THE GRAVES. PRAYERS ARE STILL BEING MUMBLED AS WE PICK OURSELVES UP FROM OUR KNEES.

WE ARE THE FIRSTBORN, SCORNED A BIT BY EVERYONE, FEARED A BIT BY EVERYONE.

The two of us drove together, and from time to time my brother put his hand on my knee. Pink Floyd was blaring out of the speakers. "The safety belt is nice and black," I said as a conciliatory gesture. Encouraged, he said that lately when Father got upset—and he was always upset with him—he began to stammer or, rather, repeat words, and it made him very angry, because it seemed just another way of blackmailing him: "There, you see, boys? That's what my life is like, that's what it's turned into, because I sacrificed it, sacrificed everything for you, for you and your sister, your brother, your mother, my career, my vital juices, my freedom, and you, and laid everything! everything! at your mother's feet! Poured it out like a Darius! . . . A Darius!" No, he is a penniless warehouse employee bent under the firm's rules and regulations and fearfully rummaging in the merchandise as if it were his—as if he were the owner!—and he hadn't received his due from the someone he was now making careful measurements for. . . . "I wouldn't go quite so far," I said, measuring myself with great care.

PRITHEE, KIND LADY, LEAVE HIM NOT. FOR WITHOUT THEE HE WILL SURELY EXPIRE. HIS BREAST CAGE WILL CAVE IN, EARTH WILL TRICKLE BETWEEN HIS RIBS—FOUL, SOUR, GRAY EARTH—AND WEEDS WILL THRUST THEIR WAY THROUGH HIS SHIRT. HIS LEGS WILL CRUMBLE, MARROW WILL OOZE FROM HIS SHINBONE, HIS SPECTACLES WILL CRACK, AND LAST BUT NOT LEAST HIS MIGHTY FOREHEAD WILL FURROW. ONLY THE BEATING OF HIS BONES WILL STILL BE AUDIBLE, MY DEAREST.

I ABSOLVE YOU OF ALL YOUR SINS, MADAM.

The mortuary had reserved two rows of benches for the family of the deceased. The four of us stood in front, staring at the wreaths and whispering now and then among ourselves. I kept a furtive eye on Father. He was strikingly handsome—a hard, white, grief-stricken stone-face. I was unnerved by his impeccable behavior. *"Hope I don't go tilt,"* my sister whispered. I made a mental note of the expression. Everything looked highly theatrical; we could even have had the leading role or at least *a* leading role, but we were so spoiled as to be ungrateful, and with the presumption of a clique of teacher's pets we sniggered snide remarks. My sister asked for my handkerchief and trumpeted into it like a man; I would later look back on the scene in disgust. M. and his wife nodded in our direction. Mother, if I remember correctly, loathed the woman. Then an old girlfriend of my brother's came up and hugged and kissed each of us in turn until she came to me. We shook hands. I was ashamed of my pomposity, but overlooked the vanity and arrogance that went with it. (She had given my brother a hard time. "We'll get back at her," Mother said softly to her sobbing son, and while he shook his head vehemently she made a sound like the cork coming out of a champagne bottle. I'll never forget it. "Back!") That non-hug stirred up quite a scandal.

FANCISKÓ AND PINTA LAID OUT MOTHER'S BODY. I SAT NEAR THE WINDOW ON A STOOL, GAZING UP AT THE PANES AND THE TREES REACHING UPWARDS BEYOND THEM. . . . FATHER SAT IN A BROWN EASY CHAIR IN THE GROWN-UPS' ROOM, SILENT. I WENT OVER TO HIM AND

PUT MY HAND ON HIS SHOULDER. "BUCK UP, OLD MAN. SOON WE'LL GO OUT FOR A WALK AND PICK UP A FEW GIRLS." "YOU THINK SO?" FATHER ASKED, LOOKING UP. "YOU THINK WE'LL HAVE ANY LUCK?"

Father's mouth kept twitching at the priest's pious inflections. Awful. I was close to tears at one point during the ceremony: when he spoke of "our deceased sister's *difficult* life." But the lives of all our brothers and sisters are generally *difficult*. Shortly thereafter they removed the wreaths, and the veils fluttered boldly. I read the name on the back of the hearse, ŠKODA, many times over. And as I walked behind the coffin, I felt as alone as if God had created the world dead, as if there were only the two of them left in the empty, yawning void: He and the dead world. As I walked behind the brown coffin shrouded in white lace, I lowered my head towards the hearse's glass box and saw my face reflected in the pane, my bare head enveloped in the white shroud.

One or another epitaph made us laugh. For those few moments we felt superior. It was drizzling. I kept slipping in the clayey soil. My poor shoes! A small hole had been made at the grave, my grandparents' grave, the size a dog digs—it too for bones. I looked up at the spreading chestnut tree and the distant, leaden sky glowering over us as it does in painfully great novels. . . . The trees stirred, and with bowed head I thought, *It doesn't matter; something had to happen.*

During the shoveling, which turned out to be much more clear-cut than I had imagined—matter-of-fact and simple, appropriate—I thought of our days as altar boys and how much we enjoyed "burying." For the money. An expert could tell with a single glance, in the twinkling of an eye, what he needed to know (from the widow's outfit, the kinds of tears, the kinds of clothes the mourners wore, the proportion of women to men and the relationship between them, etc.). . . . How much would they milk *us* for? I was clearly good for no more than ten, though with a skillful tug at the heartstrings I might go up to twenty; Father, an impeccable tipper, could be counted on for a respectable twenty a head; and my brother might go as high as a hundred. Big gentroid men on the verge of tears, we were the Chimborazos of prospects. Our sister would shoo us away languidly.

CORPSES DECOMPOSE NOISELESSLY.

They tossed the tiny mound of earth onto a filthy, frayed, and shapeless nylon sheet flapping noisily in the wind. I was as indignant as I might have been to learn that a favorite restaurant was out of heart ragout again. As soon as people came up to us with condolences, I knew Father was right: I was profoundly grateful for every handshake, for the shallowest of words. There were some German speakers among them; the foreign language sounded crude under the circumstances, especially from such refined-looking specimens: they seemed to be saying that despite the uncommon, unusual, unbelievably obscene character of it all there was "nothing wrong." Yet something was very definitely wrong: our mother had died.

Seeing all the people, I automatically thought how I'd give the customary report at home about "the events": "Everything went well, Mother. A big crowd . . . nothing special." I hardly noticed there was something a little off.

My sister stepped on the white ribbon from the wreath and even got tangled in it. Her sulky, resentful face kept popping into view. I watched the silk ribbon being pressed into the mud.

GORY IN EXCELSIS DEO!
TIME FOR A CELEBRATION! BY "CELEBRATION" WE MEAN NEITHER ELEGANCE NOR FASHION; WE MEAN DIGNITY, COMPOSURE, LOFTY MORALS, LIGHT NOT LUSTER, GOLD NOT RICHES.

The cold cuts, the astute selection of drinks, the placement of the napkins—it was almost as if Mother were still alive. Almost. Because now I noticed the refinement that had gone unnoticed before; I even noticed the color of the new napkins, the needless extravagance of the cold plates. Weeds had begun to sprout—the first in an endless series of changes. I don't know which I found more painful: the infuriating sameness or the infuriating difference.

There was a big crowd: *we have a large family*—ourselves and the close relatives (much-loved and less-loved aunts and the like) followed by more distant ones, strangers in whom we were surprised to see our own gestures like stolen goods, though we merely laughed together at the prank and called their sons and daughters cousins. "Dearest cousin," I said to a dark, willowy girl, lithe and supple as an animal. "Karin." The back of her dress plunged all the way to the posterior, revealing a fine, dark shimmer at the hip level. Was it minutes, was it years I stood there? I cannot say.

On the suburban train the other day, in the muffled roar that makes you think you catch your neighbors' conversation whereas in fact you catch nothing, I suddenly heard a young woman's spiteful voice ring out behind me, saying, "ARE YOU OUT OF YOUR MIND?! DON'T *YOU* BE THE ONE TO KILL HIM!" In the same way my relatives' words cut through unexpectedly, like a knife "someone" points at your stomach while you're peacefully doing the dishes. Behind me I heard "not if you paid me" and somebody's sergeant was a "very human human being." I had to laugh, though I was scared stiff, cowering in a corner. I made sure to catch a glimpse of them when I got off: nothing special, just like you and me. Fantastic!

THE LAY OF THE OCEAN: SHE LAY IN STATE ON THE SOFA AS IF FLYING WITHOUT WINGS. THE FAMILY IDIOT TORE OFF THE QUILT. "NOW AT LEAST YOU CAN SEE WHAT MAN AMOUNTS TO!" I SAW: HER TWO WHITE BREASTS ABSURDLY SWOLLEN, THE HAIR ON THE MONS VENERIS IRREVERENTLY VIGOROUS, THE WHOLE BODY WILDLY ALIVE, ALL BUT THE CHIN, WHICH HAD FALLEN ONTO THE NECK. WAS IT MINUTES, WAS IT YEARS I STOOD THERE? I CANNOT SAY. "REALLY NOW! IN FRONT OF THE CHILD!" THE EARTH EXCLAIMED, CALLING ME BACK. THE SUN WAS ABOUT TO SMOTHER THE ROOM IN GOLD.

If we talked about the "dearly departed," it was perhaps because our much maligned and, between you and me, much loved good manners made us feel it would be tactless not to; it would be like neglecting her simply because she . . . *wasn't present,* because she was passé. Her doctor explained with a smile that Mother just wouldn't die; he presented it the way enlightened parents boast about a madcap and therefore engaging little whim on the part of their child, and more or less hinted that the *solution* would clearly have been to . . . "But she wouldn't." "You mean, she had a will?"

Karin and a woman I didn't know were standing by the piano. "My life, the world, men" were the only words of her English I could catch. They were enjoying each other a bit too much. I was gripped by ineffable longing. The woman I didn't know was surrounded on all sides by solicitous concern. "Hello," she said to me. I froze. "I see you don't know who I am. I'm Saca, or rather"—she gave a hoarse laugh and was suddenly old—"Aunt Saca, and you've known me since you were . . . Don't be scared, don't be scared! You used to sit on my lap." A few people laughed. "Oh, that Saca . . ." "I'm not scared," I said, and I wasn't. Suddenly everyone was silent.

Of course the poor soul had to be fed towards the end, but how gracefully she accepted her helplessness! Just like my poor Ödön (who suffered so at the slightest hint of filth, *you remember how* soigné *he was*) when they pulled out his intestine and his . . . his feces dripped down right there, next to the bed. When I've finished with you, my dear, you'll forget you ever worked in the *medical profession.* But later, when we stayed up all night together at Ödön's bedside, you came up from behind, put your arms around me, and said, "You must hate me," to which my husband replied, "You may be certain she does not, my girl; it's against her religion," which is true. . . . And now our dear (or poor?) Lizi, who looked so young because her spirit stayed young. God, how exasperating or, rather, irritating to see her grow old—not her body (because she aged gracefully, wore her wrinkles with dignity almost, and grayed in an interesting way, though in the end her hair began to fall out) but altogether: she bore the weight of her increasing years with equanimity, except for a brief hysterical period when she went around in a copper-colored wig, broad sash, and Indian veils, as "Vengerovskaya, the local beauty queen," though perhaps it was because she thought wisdom comes with age and it was her bounden duty to share it with her loved ones, call their attention to the inconsistencies of a life lived, the periodic miseries of the spiritual horizon, "What sort of life is that, *my child!?*" and so on (while she of course grew pettier and pettier, upset by anything she wasn't used to, tightfisted [!] and preachy and constantly predisposed to see the bad in everything).

SUDDENLY HE REALIZED WHY HIS MOTHER HAD HATED SPIDERS THEN, WHY SHE WAS *NERVOUS* WHENEVER HE CODDLED THEM—ESPECIALLY THE DADDY LONGLEGS—AND SET THEM LOOSE.

IT WAS THE WEB!

The sun was about to smother the room in gold. A smell of tar, the gentle rustle of scarlet plane trees, autumn in the rooms, frost and smoke, the muffled murmur of a stone house, an ugly rat gnawing on doors and flour bins. "Not a *pretty corpse,*" said the doctor, sucking on his empty cigarette holder. Streaming blue-black hair, a sharp, short but not pug nose (an adolescent's nose), a strong, aggressive chin—in short, the sort of man who needs to shave twice a day. Again and again I was amazed at how small he was. It was the legs that did it. "What do you want from me?" I cried. He laughed. "Let me see your glasses," he said, reaching over. I meant to pull my head away, but stood there motionless. He removed the glasses carefully, as though undressing me, and I cooperated quite willingly. He held my head in his hands and said, "You look good like this."

I don't want to make these notes seem hyperrealistic, but the toilet is the first thing in the bathroom, right near the door—my head was a few inches from the door. I heard steps; I checked the flow. A rhythmic breathing noise, a light panting, a puffing filtered through the keyhole. "Is you?" Karin's voice. I didn't answer. "I know is you! I know! I know is you in there!" More steps. *"Was tust du hier?!"* It was Saca. *"Lass mich! Lass mich endlich! Das geht dich nichts an!"* A tussle?

The comedy of my fumbling complications blind to the simplicities of her lust. Shadows, night, silence, cold.

I am tempted. Wouldn't it be better in this instance to quiver? *Voilà votre mort, monsieur!* The women snuggle up, their hair shrieking as it touches; they whisper, their breaths becoming one. The filling has dropped out of the stuffed bread. Mother's recipe, scarcely spoiled. Karin had a refined, foreign scent. In the dark I could see only her arm—bright and shiny, good and strong, nice and fleshy—a brown, summer arm. When I dropped my hands, hopeless, into my lap—still feigning illness—the girl took them as Mother used to. I was so grateful I'd have done anything she asked. God, I'm shallow when it comes to these things.

"COME INTO THE MEN'S TOILET WITH ME." FINGER MET SLIT, AND THERE WAS A MOAN OF "OH GOD!" MY FATHER IS ATTENDING A CLASS IN GOOD BEHAVIOR. "DO THE MEN RISE WHEN FRIENDS GREET US WHILE WE ARE SITTING IN A BOOTH?" "THE MEN DO NOT RISE WHEN THEY ARE SEATED IN A BOOTH," HE ANSWERS, "ALTHOUGH THEY MAY HALF-RISE AND MAKE APOLOGIES FOR NOT FULLY RISING."

With a superior smile the doctor gave his empty cigarette holder another twist. "What is life? Let me tell you. When you're born, you have three and only three lives to choose from: go to the right and the wolves will eat you; go to the left and you'll eat the wolves; go straight ahead and you'll eat yourself." I made no reply. "The only thing that consoles us in our misery is amusement. Amusement distracts us and leads us imperceptibly to death. There is no balm for death, misery, or ignorance. If we are to have a happy life, we must find a way not to think of them."

How I hated this ambiguous speech, and what pleasure I found in it. My face flushed, I began breathing heavily: the proportions had shifted. "Have a drink," he ordered. "Then we can clear out of this place." He told me about two nurses, *zwei Schwestern,* who were always ready for a good time, always laughing, never in the dumps; when they rubbed their thighs together you heard music, and they'd row, too, flap their arms in the sand like coots. "Come on," he said, "let's go." "I don't understand, I don't understand, I don't understand!" I cried. "Calm down," he said. "Everybody and everybody's everybody dies." And he laid a light, cool hand on my forehead.

I went out for brandy; the mourning fox took off. The face of the cloakroom attendant was gleaming with grease. Especially the lips. The kind of thing you usually see only in fashion magazines. She may have been pretty at one time, and powerful; now she was old—but I added to myself—and pretty and powerful. I felt almost dizzy; I had ten thousand minds and no weight, no conscience—just nerves. Sand in the wind. I watched her work. She always knew who had paid and who hadn't. "How?" "I turn up the hem. Then smooth it down." She lifted the cloakroom ticket to my face, her breast rising and falling like a bellows. "So you smooth it down . . ." "I smooth it down." "Really? Is that how?" "I don't know what you're thinking." "I'm thinking what I can." "No need to worry," she said with an almost contemptuous pout. "I'll be back tomorrow." "Fine. Though I can tell you won't be." "How do you know?" "I can tell you need everything at once."

PUPPET.

The tears crept up within me like a repulsive beast. A shaggy, soggy lump, like a skunk. Or a jackal pup. Or an *obese* rat. Large, empty halls took turns inside me with black, heavy halls. The corridors connecting them are bowels. My stomach will not stop rumbling. All I can think of is fine food, *côte de veau aux truffes*. There's a sewer smell inside me. No, there isn't. No, there isn't. There's nothing. There's a mother. Mother wearing her purple silver-stitched negligee, the broad Chinese sash, the silk slippers, and, in her ebony black hair, the ravishing rainbow-colored headdress. Mirage, constant wind, the tiny glass pendants of Viennese chandeliers clinking together—wind, breeze, breath. Doesn't it frighten you, my boy? Oh, Mother, if I dared answer all truth and no tact, I'd say no, I don't understand your question, how could I be frightened by what exists, isn't what is not more frightening, the not that is, the is that is not, sh, sh, quiet, silly boy, bad boy. Quiet.

SHE STANDS WITH HER LEGS SPREAD WIDE, THE TWO SMALLEST ONES HUGGING HER KNEES. THEY REACH UP BETWEEN HER THIGHS AND SCRATCH. SHE BRUSHES THEM AWAY, DISTRACTED.

GOD BLEW GOLD ONTO MY HEART.

The white-smocked nurses might just as well have been wearing miniskirts. They were a little frightened by the brandy smell. "Where have you been, you naughty boys?" the plumper of the two asked at last. I stared spellbound at the tiny silver panties glowing in the darkness at the base of her thighs. "Silver's my favorite color," she said proudly. Hearing her fragmentary confession, my fingers playing shamelessly with a cigarette, I felt a rush of friendliness and decided to humiliate her. I went and danced with the other one. "I don't drink; I'm coarse when I drink." She laughed at me, and I laughed back. She gave me a vigorous kiss. She used an East German toothpaste. That was when I recognized her. She was the one who had pointed out Mother to us in the hospital! I was unable to revive my former hatred for her, however; I needed a new one.

The doctor drank from the bottle as he danced. "Bubbly, o bubbly," he sang lustily. "Death is something you have to want!" "Who the hell wants death!" whooped the girl in his arms. "Everything's just fine, baby," said the nurse with a quick pat on the cheek, almost by way of apology. Suddenly it seemed so *insufficient,* cool, bodiless, contrived; I felt like screaming, whining! More, more, more! I bored my forehead into her burning neck, flung my arms around her, and squeezed and squeezed. "What's wrong?" she asked. "I . . . I . . . ," I began, "I . . ." I realized I was crying. "Poor baby." But then I felt from a slight tensing of her muscles that she was about to pull away. "Don't, please don't," I begged in terror. "Don't what?" she asked mindlessly.

We were standing in an alcove near the window; my legs were shaking. She looked out into the darkness, but all she could see was my reflection. As she turned, I saw she was afraid. That made me want her so much it felt like a spasm in my gut. "Don't be afraid," I said with hostility. "If you leave me alone now, I'll kill you!" Take me into thy night, o abbess.

THOU ART THAT THOU MIGHT BE.
MAKE ME, MAKE ME FREE!
TERROR . . . ATION. MAY THY VULVA SHINE ITS COUNTENANCE UPON ME! CLITORIS PECCATA MUNDI!

"The sky is bare," the doctor said cheerfully, "the house in despair; there is no laughter anywhere." Then he launched into a tired disquisition, constantly interrupted by hiccups and snorts, on sexual intercourse, on what makes a great passion, namely, an ever more impersonal plunge, an all-consuming fall, the impersonality of which was both terrifying and enticing, terrifying because someone is lost, the "I" we so love, and enticing: to be anyone, to want everything. But can you want everything? That is the question. His intelligent eyes shone sadly now. "See what I mean?"

There was no one left on the porch. A deep, dark night hung over us, bright stars shone in the windswept, wind-chiseled sky, and a twinkling light in the distance infused it with a spray of briefly vanishing ashes. The breeze wafted the scent of spice and stone several streets farther, shooting past like a car in a long skid on a wet road; immediately thereafter confused shouts from the distance pierced the silence, which then, sky and stars, descended upon us with its full weight.

No one who lives can hide. Given time, everything happens to a man. Time the miser is shrinking.

PIERROT <LE FOU> IS FEELING SAD. HE CLEARLY REGRETS HIS PARIS PRANKS, OR IS IT FEAR OF REVENGE? HE PLUCKS GOLD-PAPER FLOWERS AND SCATTERS THEM IN THE RISING EVENING WIND.... SUDDENLY THERE IS A LOUD ROAR NEARBY. THE EARTH BEGINS TO QUAKE, THE ROAR GROWS INTO THUNDER AND MOVES CLOSER AND CLOSER, AND A MAGNIFICENT HERALDIC LION WITH A

GOLD-DUST MANE STEPS OUT OF A LEAFY BOWER. TERRIFIED, PIERROT TOSSES THE REST OF HIS FLOWERS TO THE WINDS AND TRIES TO FLEE, BUT JUMPING A BARRIER HE GETS STUCK LIKE A HALF-OPEN PENKNIFE AND HIS TROUSERS BURST WITH AN INDECENT BANG IN AT LEAST A HUNDRED PLACES. THE HERALDIC LION, LOOKING ON WITH AN IRONIC SMILE, DAINTILY REMOVES ITS GLOVES AND PROCEEDS TO VIOLATE THE HELPLESSLY DANGLING PIERROT....

THE PUBLIC IS AMAZED AT THE BOLDNESS OF IT ALL.

"You can go now," said the doctor. There was an old man gardening in front of the house; his head cocked to one side, he was examining a bushy-rooted plant, holding it away from his body as if it were a kitten he'd seized by the scruff of the neck. Words come to mind when I think of words, and vice versa. *If I feel rootless, it is because I am the root.* And again I am visited by the image of a woman standing over me on all fours, breasts hanging, rear end wiggling vigorously, breasts dangling, pubic root system jutting out between the legs—a delicate, mysterious shadow thrown onto a water-stained wall.

And there in front of the house, in the shady garden, as I gazed on that peculiar carrion-like plant-animal in a sinewy old hand, feeling empty, dusty, headachy, far gone!, excluded from all roles, nothing of my role—being natural—remaining but to acknowledge, within myself, to myself, by myself: I am an orphan.

And at that very moment—with all the force and self-evident clarity produced by the solution of a mathematics problem that had once dawned on me, unexpectedly, after three days' work, while I was having my morning bacon, yes, me, *le phénix de la famille*—the stooped, skyscraping figure of an old architect friend appeared. With loose-limbed, even ungainly gesticulations he offered me a seat in his dark, fragile apartment, his dressing gown and handsome silk scarf indicating he had made special preparations for the occasion. It was the first time I was paying him a personal visit, though I had known his buildings for as long as I can remember, for so long and with such intimacy that *this* meeting might merely have been an (important) extra. Time flew by with this and that; we might have known each other a thousand years, two old ladies, two old crones, sitting there knitting, exchanging tricks of the trade, KNIT ONE, PURL TWO, when with unfathomable fury and at the same time full of shame, he said, "I'm a widower!" after which he spoke—with unbearably long pauses yet connectedly, his eyes sparkling, his voice full of emotion, the words sometimes so obstructing one another, so jumbled, that I worried for the edifice of language itself—about how he felt or rather *thought* that he had been to blame for his wife's death, that he was to blame because he had made his peace with it, accepted it, accepted a practice everyone accepts merely because it is supported by millennia of potbellied authority, that is, that his wife was mortal like everyone else, yes, he had submitted to it like a cowardly coyote, though what halfway free, quarter-way self-respecting Hungarian court would accept it as evidence? Not a one. That man is mortal is just hearsay and hearsay doesn't stand up in court, so he had criminally neglected certain fundamental obligations, he had fallen for it, fallen for their trickery like a babe in the woods, they had duped him, bamboozled him, pulled the wool over his eyes. . . . He swallowed hard a few times and gasped mutely for breath as though struggling for words before the fact, words he feared, mistrusted, yet used, feverishly waving his arms in the air, his handsome, virile face twitching on and off and a wild woman occasionally peering out of it. He shouldn't have let such a mean thing happen; he should have—he brushed away a tear—he should have . . . he should simply have lain down next to her, put his arms around her, hugged her, stroked her, caressed her, fondled her, and held on to her, clasped, squeezed, kneaded her until she either crumbled in his hands or came to life. . . . O the mud! . . . the mud! . . . (Dear old friend. I love you.)

ON THE BURNING FEBRUARY MORNING WHEN BEATRIZ VITERBO DIED, AFTER AN IMPERIOUS DEATH AGONY THAT REFUSED EVEN FOR A MOMENT TO SINK INTO SENTIMENTALITY OR FEAR, I NOTED THAT THE BILLBOARDS IN PLAZA CONSTITUCIÓN DISPLAYED A NEW CIGARETTE ADVERTISEMENT; IT MADE ME SAD, BECAUSE I REALIZED THAT THE VAST AND INCESSANTLY CHANGING UNIVERSE HAD BEGUN TO MOVE AWAY FROM HER AND THAT THIS CHANGE WAS THE FIRST IN AN INFINITE SERIES.

THE UNIVERSE WILL CHANGE BUT NOT I, I THOUGHT WITH THE VANITY OF MELANCHOLY; THERE WERE TIMES, I KNEW, WHEN MY VAIN DEVOTION HAD EXASPERATED HER; NOW THAT SHE WAS DEAD, I COULD DEDICATE MYSELF TO HER MEMORY, WITHOUT HOPE, THOUGH WITHOUT HUMILIATION EITHER.

Not on your life! I said. Neglect like that is something I . . . No, I refuse. The garden was suddenly transformed; the lawn, larks, and poppies were suddenly like a bowl filled with pitch-black cream. . . . I heard a panting noise growing faster and faster, I heard an animal rutting close behind me, rough, bloody. I skated down the hospital corridors with the abandon of a cartoon character and the serendipitous triumph of Till Eulenspiegel on the frozen Flemish (?) canals.

Suddenly Mother was there before me. On her side, see-through white, huddled up, almost hugging her knees. Her forehead had grown. It somehow made her face look girlish. A curious little girl, pressing her forehead to the shop window. Her hands shivering with cold on her shoulders. Her grayish hair sticking to her forehead.

Who is it, anyway, who is it lying there—thing, form, gray blob in black hole? And so familiar . . . A dear friend . . .

"Mother dear, can't you hear me, Mother, Beatriz, Beatriz Elena, Beatriz Elena Viterbo, Beatriz my darling, my lost and gone forever Beatriz, it is I, I am here . . ."

The cells are going out into the world! I can tell. I can tell by the closed, motionless eyes, by the deep, dark pits all around, by the weals, the oversized forehead, the nose that seems to stand aloof like a stuck-on afterthought, and the swollen belly, and not so much the graying hair as the hair's unexpected straightness, all the life has gone out of it, it's greasy and matted, and it hangs over the pitted gray surface called the cheek by "the ever-bored,

ever-mournful postmortem-master." Her feet were still warm!!!
NOT SO MUCH THAT AS . . . IT CONSOLES ME AS A MAN IS CONSOLED BY HIS MOTHER. O MY POOR MOURNING BROTHER! THE ONLY SON OF THIS FINE WOMAN NOW RESTING IN HER GRAVE, YOU KNOW WHAT A MOTHER'S CONSOLATION MEANS FOR US.

I am become as sounding brass, or a tinkling cymbal! I hope you all rot. I hate you.

A bloody porridge, that's what this garden is. No, no, no, no! Burgeon in me, O Lord!

My son. My little son. My darling little son. So that's how it is, you there, me here, me here, you there, I don't think at all. I've accepted your death mindless and wordless. You have died, and I am no more. And so on. You no longer exist, yet you are. You are: the one who died. You and only you are the one who died. My tears have dried now, but whenever I think about being your mother, whenever I think, *I* am your mother, I am moved by my own self. The thought of you numbs me so I'm sometimes startled I don't drop the things I've been holding.

You wouldn't like the following sentence (because it's tactless and much too self-important): I think of you so you can think of me. I feel no pain, only fatigue, frailty, and growing horror. *Cracks:* now we could call it all pain. As usual I answer bad questions with silence. I'm unable to articulate my condition. Too much goes on between two movements, and in the intervals, sorry, my bowels seem to gush. (I shall no longer apologize for matters of style.)

I am incapable of grasping a single day's events in a single day. That is very bad. *There is no place I should wish to be.* Though none other in all the world . . .

I STEPPED OUT OF MY DOOR
AND THEN LOOKED EASTWARDS,
AND THERE I SPIED A CHAPEL WHITE AND FAIR,
COMPASSIONATE WITHOUT,

PURE GOLD WITHIN.
WHY DOST THOU WEEP, O MOTHER DEAR?
O SON, MY SON, BELOVED SAINTED SON,
I DID NOT BEAR THEE TO BECOME
THE SUFF'RING MOTHER!

HE WHO SAYS THIS PRAYER BOTH MORN AND NIGHT
SHALL SEE THE VIRGIN MARY ERE HE DIE.

I'm mourning for you! Wearing black stockings, a big black hat, and an ugly black suit. I'll be an old woman in my mourning, and that's a real sacrifice on my part, believe me. I'm mourning for you whether you like it or not. I'm no nobody if my grief is great. I'm in trouble; I stare in the mirror to console myself. My face flashes unexpectedly, a burly bird. I demand special privileges, respect: I have a corpse!

I believe you always liked to think I wasn't your "good mother."

Yesterday I forgot to eat. I didn't venture out until evening, not till evening, as if there were a war on. . . . I went to see Ágnes. We hugged silently. I cried. I could feel her warmth against my ribs. . . . I could have held you forever, dear Ágnes, stayed in your arms forever.

Time is a beautiful, white, weary woman. She draws her feet under her pleated silk skirt, a bitter sneer on her immobile face. Something has happened, so it's over. Though that's not clear. In the best of casts she'd be played by Edith Clever. If she were a man, she'd be reeking of brandy and sobbing. She sits there with great strength. "I am alone, my son, and when you're alone you're old. But even then I'm not old!!!"

See? I'm as open as a wound, I whimper, I whine. I'm so soft I could fall in love at any moment. Not a pretty sight. I'm of low-grade ingredients, my boy. . . . The fall! that hovers on the border between frailty and sin. It has no sign.

In the morning, half asleep, I rolled onto the crumpled quilt and pressed it with my thighs. Cry! I want you to. In other words: *May your eyes fill with tears. . . .*

When I was at Ágnes's, I ate half a chicken without

sitting down. She'd done a good job of roasting it, and the crunchy red brown skin was nice and sticky. I was still sucking my fingers on the stairs and didn't dare touch my face though the salty tears nipped my skin.

I'm not sad. Or happy either. I have no feeling. Only the pain remains. In spite of everything. The same pain, the same fear . . . and so it's never easier, never harder. Everything is worse and worse.

HELPING VERBS MAY EXPRESS NEGATION.

I'm afraid in this country, my son. I might be afraid in other countries, but this happens to be the one where I'm afraid. Not very, a little. You think fear can't be measured. Well, it can; I've read about it. And anyway, the fact that fear is petty doesn't make itself felt until after the fact, after it's *been* petty. By which time it's ridiculous to rejoice. Or at least frightening.

IT IS A WORLD WHICH MAINTAINS IT HAS HONOR AND IN WHICH PEOPLE MAINTAIN THERE IS HONOR, YET WHERE QUITE PLAINLY THERE IS NO HONOR LEFT OR, RATHER, WHERE THERE HAS NEVER BEEN ANYTHING REMOTELY SIMILAR, AND IT IS NOT ONLY A FEARFUL AND FEAR-PROVOKING WORLD BUT A RIDICULOUS ONE, THOUGH THAT WE LIVE IN A FEARFUL, FEAR-PROVOKING, AND RIDICULOUS WORLD IS SOMETHING WE EACH HAVE TO COME TO TERMS WITH, AND HOW MANY HUNDREDS OF THOUSANDS, HOW MANY MILLIONS OF PEOPLE HAVE NOT COME TO TERMS WITH IT, HE THOUGHT, ESPECIALLY IN THIS HOPELESSLY FEARFUL, FEAR-PROVOKING, AND RIDICULOUS COUNTRY, HIS FATHERLAND, THE MOST FEARFUL AND RIDICULOUS OF ALL COUNTRIES. TO BE ABLE TO EXIST IN THIS COUNTRY, HIS FATHERLAND, TO GET ALONG FOR EVEN A DAY, ONE CAN NEVER TELL THE TRUTH TO ANYONE ABOUT ANYTHING, BECAUSE LIES AND LIES ALONE KEEP THINGS MOVING IN THIS COUNTRY, LIES WITH ALL THEIR VEILS AND FLOURISHES AND DISGUISES AND INTIMIDATIONS. LIES ARE EVERYTHING IN THIS COUNTRY; TRUTH EARNS YOU NOTHING BUT ACCUSATIONS, CONDEMNATIONS, AND SCORN. THAT IS WHY HE, CSÁTH, DID NOT CONCEAL THE FACT THAT HIS ENTIRE NATION HAD TAKEN REFUGE IN LIES. ANYONE WHO TELLS THE TRUTH IS LIABLE TO PUNISHMENT AND RIDICULE; THE MASSES OR THE COURTS DETERMINE WHETHER TO MAKE A MAN LIABLE TO PUNISHMENT OR

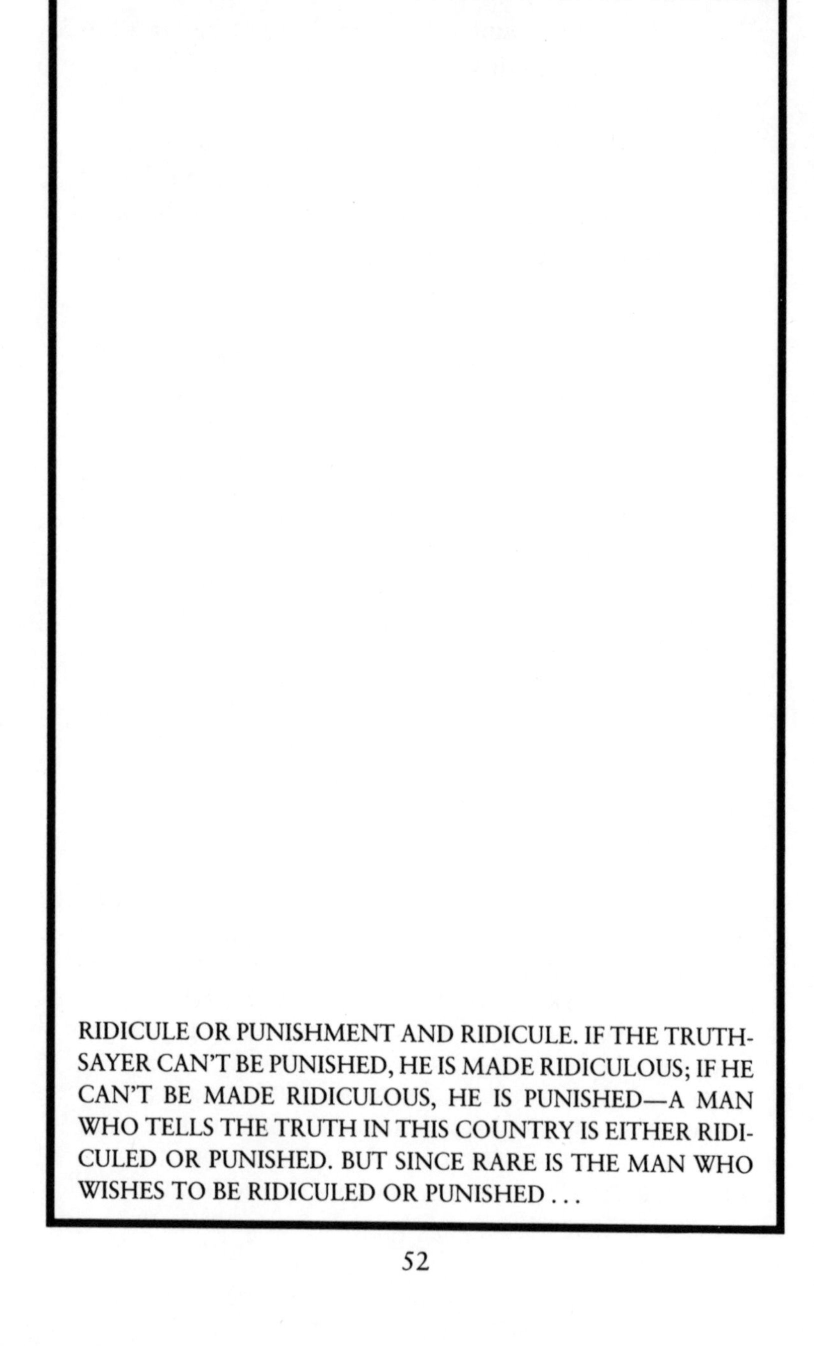
RIDICULE OR PUNISHMENT AND RIDICULE. IF THE TRUTH-SAYER CAN'T BE PUNISHED, HE IS MADE RIDICULOUS; IF HE CAN'T BE MADE RIDICULOUS, HE IS PUNISHED—A MAN WHO TELLS THE TRUTH IN THIS COUNTRY IS EITHER RIDICULED OR PUNISHED. BUT SINCE RARE IS THE MAN WHO WISHES TO BE RIDICULED OR PUNISHED . . .

Your father happened to be working on his never-to-be-finished manuscript when some soldiers came looking for Germans. They were young, almost children; they burst in with a great hullabaloo, shouting, rushing around, and we had no way of knowing whether they were raging mad or simply having a wild time of it. Your father knows Russian, even if he denies it, and barely looking up from the manuscript he bade the officers welcome and told them to make themselves at home, though he didn't insist on it and was, in fact, as they could see, quite busy. Working on a kind of novel. *Writing* a novel, that is. That's right: *roman, povest'*. The boy in charge turned bright red and began ranting and raving about how while they had been up to their knees in blood, mowing down the enemy—and God knows, it was no picnic—your father had sat here arrogantly, no, brazenly, scribbling. And with that he grabbed the pile of manuscript pages and hurled it into the fire. It burned.

Your father shrieked and gave the downy-chinned soldier a slap in the face.

Then there was silence, fragile and bare. The boy headed for the door as if it were over, but turned back in a flash and motioned "Come with me" with his head. When your father went up to him, he said softly, almost pleasantly, like someone determined to be polite, "We're going to shoot you."

Just then a Hungarian officer burst in—*must have switched sides or something* and cheeky as they come—and asked what was going on and all. Well, naturally your father was scared, but fear loosened his tongue, gave him the courage to light into the officer. "Who do you think you are, anyway? Who do you think you are, fooling with death, giving it, taking it? What makes you think you can do anything you like?" "Who's to stop us?" "God, for one." "There is no God." "Satan then." The officer laughed. "If there's no God, there's no Satan." "Fine, just fine. Perfect. Maybe there is no God, maybe there is no Satan, maybe there's nothing, nothing at all, just you, nothing but you. Perfect. . . . But then you're a bunch of bastards! Damn you to the end of time!"

The soldiers were tired, tired more of the situation as a whole than of your father. They cursed and left. Your father stood there sobbing. Oh, how he loved his scenes. Meanwhile I was trembling inside the wardrobe, afraid they'd f..k me. Even now the smell of mothballs makes me retch.

"GOD BLESS FATHER," HE THOUGHT ON HIS FATHER'S BIRTHDAY. "ALL THINGS CONSIDERED, HIS VIRTUES ARE UNDYING." "HEY THERE, TOUSLEHEAD! WHERE'S YOUR MAMA?"

I have no talent; I conclude as much from your death. Sorry.

I dreamed I kissed you on your deathbed, my son. Your mouth had sunk like an old grave or an old woman's, and you wheezed each time you inhaled. The wheezing increased when I kissed you, kissed you lightly, and you suddenly started gasping for air and a caterpillar as thick as an arm crawled out of your mouth. *This big.* The caterpillar had a large, light green head, the same color as the faded cover of Győző Határ's Sterne translation in the 1955 edition, and it laughed like that cabaret artist—you know who I mean—his name of course escapes me for the moment.

A laughing green caterpillar. *How will it end, my son?* I was terribly ashamed.

I have a composer friend—well, I don't know him all that well, but I think of him as a friend—and he can look as anxious and encouraging as a child lost among coats in a closet. . . . I was going up the broad staircase at the Music Academy, and he was standing at the head of the stairs; I went up to him from behind as if he were a wall, stood next to him, and put my hand on his shoulder as if I were a man. "Well," I said. "Aha," he said. "Are you well?" I asked. "I am," he said, "and you?" "Me? No."

There was a girl sitting next to me at the concert. When she took off her sweater—it was warm—her blouse slid up and I could see the small of her back. Her skin was tan and radiant. Unable to resist, I reached through the gap between the back of the seat and the pillow and touched her with the tip of a finger. "I

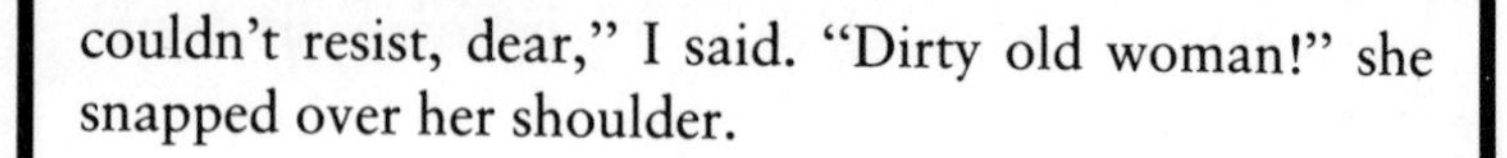
couldn't resist, dear," I said. "Dirty old woman!" she snapped over her shoulder.

"ENOUGH OF THIS TORPID EXISTENCE! WRITE DOWN YOUR DREAMS EVERY MORNING, ADDING NOTHING, BUT LEAVING NOTHING OUT. WHAT DO YOU SAY? WE'LL MAKE A BOOK OUT OF THEM—I'LL DO THE GRAPHICS—AND THE MONEY WILL COME ROLLING IN!" HE PUT HIS ARM AROUND HIS MOTHER, AND HE WAS ABOUT TO UP AND TWIRL HER TO THE RHYTHM OF AN IMAGINARY WALTZ WHEN SHE UPPED AND STOPPED HIM.

I've always hated writing. Because I always knew what was happening to me. And if nothing happened, I accepted that too. But now . . . it's like binding my own hands. . . . Everything closes in on me—like those nighttime flowers, snapdragons or whatever they're called—and I have no freedom, I don't write what I want, I write what I can, what the sentence permits. For instance, it sometimes helps to put things in the past or the plural. Unbelievable!

No matter how I twist it and deplorable as it is, my writing grows out of your death. My dreams are regularly visited by a brazen devil, a lascivious little creature, like a Murillo putto. In full color too: hoofs of sparkling yellow horn, a sensual, scarlet mouth, and a fine film of silk saliva—I can see it now, squatting on my stomach.

Sometimes I'm sorry you're so modest. Or rather such a prude—you do confuse the two. I'd really like to have a talk with you, my son. A frank talk. I'm curious about everything, and as you know, as I think you know, I'm no coward (though I'm not courageous either), I'm not afraid of myself. (Nor *I* of you, I'd have said, if *you* had said it.)

Naturally the devil squatting on my stomach made occasional grabs to the groin, after which it would grow serious and hiss repugnantly in my face, "You monster, you! Don't think I don't know that even in your hour of woe you're worried about wording!"

Waking up tired in the morning my hand between my thighs. Don't blush, my son. You were there too. . . . (My poor father once caught me playing with myself. Why not read a book instead? he said calmly. Whereupon I exploded, "What has *that* got to do with dearest

Pater's bloody books?" But he didn't beat me; he simply left the room in silence.) Anyway, lots of green, the dying pink of the tamarisk blossom, the curly black devil with the big red mouth. People think you're a puritan. It's your reputation. We know how far off the mark they are.

I WRITE IN THE THIRD PERSON SINGULAR. IT MAKES ME FEEL SAFE. I HOPE I WON'T DIE QUITE SO SOON.

When I was a child, everything happened in the garden. Four arborvitaes stood at the four corners of a path surrounding a circular clearing. See, my boy? The squaring of the circle! Those arborvitaes were marvelous—not mere trees, no, beings of a higher order all their own. I knew them well, and they accepted my enthusiasm gracefully, for they were wise old men in whom the ravages of time, with its tumultuous giving and taking, were scarcely visible. They and their green turbulence were the picture of life to me; I think I knew their every twig.

The tree to the upper right! I could sit under its thick, low branches on a soft, silken, and dazzlingly green carpet of moss and there imagine everything. Good, good, cool and hot. I would hear Mama's voice calling me whenever I pleased, and I felt a special pleasure—special because malicious—at watching the French governess's face, fury red, as she stood by the gigantic white double doors of the semicircular terrace, stamped her feet, waved her arms, and then, fed up with waiting—I could see it all!—walked slowly back to the "fancy" stall. . . . Father dismissed her before long. "A flighty one she was," he said once during supper to my mother. We went on eating in silence, which Father suddenly broke again with the words, "But what a fine pronunciation she had." Your grandmother made no reply.

THE CHURCH FAIR FORTUNE-TELLERS RESERVED THEIR SERIOUS FUTURES FOR THE PALMS OF YOUNG MEN; A WOMAN'S FUTURE WAS A JOKE. NO PROSPECTS, EVERYTHING PLANNED IN ADVANCE: SOME PLAYFUL FLIRTING,

SOME GIGGLES, A BRIEF BEWILDERMENT, AND THEN THE FIRST ALIEN, DISCIPLINED LOOK OF A WOMAN GOING BACK TO KEEPING HOUSE, THE FIRST CHILDREN, A SHORT BREAK AFTER WORKING HARD IN THE KITCHEN, IGNORED FROM THE START AND INCREASINGLY INCLINED TO IGNORE, TALKS TO HERSELF, HAS TROUBLE KEEPING ON HER FEET, HAS VARICOSE VEINS, NEVER SAYS A WORD, ONLY MUMBLES IN HER SLEEP, HAS CANCER OF THE UTERUS, AND WITH DEATH THE PLAN COMES TO FRUITION. IT WAS ALL THERE IN THE SQUARES OF A GAME THE GIRLS IN OUR NEIGHBORHOOD PLAY: PALE/TIRED/WEAK/ ILL/DEAD.

Mama often gave the children's ears and nostrils a quick clean with her saliva as she walked past. I always recoiled; I didn't like the saliva smell.

We were mountain climbing once with a group of friends when she started off to the side of the road to relieve nature. I was ashamed of her and began to bawl, so she held it in.

The egg liqueur bottle in the sideboard!

They would churn the butter and put fresh mulberry leaves next to it. The adjutants had dinner with us every Sunday. I know exactly where in the garden I learned the Thirteenth Psalm. Your Uncle Miklós gave Feri Székesi pee for beer. We got a pony. The Austrian aide-de-camp designate peeled the crisp skin off the suckling pig, handed it to the chambermaid, and said, *"Bitte noch einmal braten!"* Lajos Mondvai once crawled into a freshly made bed in his dirty boots while we were playing hide-and-seek. When I had a toothache, they rubbed my gums with rum. "Want to play doctor?" I whispered to the teacher's six-year-old son in the shed, but I got caught. We had two fox terriers called Muki and Missy. When Mitzi, our fawn, stuck her snout out, Muki bit it half off and the vet had to come and sew it back together. Papa gave Muki a terrible thrashing. We hated coffee with cream, so we'd pour gobs of sugar into it and send it back as too sweet. "The desk seems to be missing from the invertory, sir." "Well, here's a fart; put *that* in your 'invertory.' " (A rolltop desk! The cat's whiskers!) Even seasonal workers were entitled to bacon. Guszti Bucsányi cut a fine figure with his mustache. We went skating in winter when the pond froze over. Zsiga Papp was the fastest; his breeches had four or five buttons beneath the knee. When Kornél Günther was a threshing inspector, he bet he could eat ten kilos of watermelon in two hours. He won the bet by sitting in a large vat of water and eating and peeing for two hours straight. *That was the solution!*

FURTHERMORE, THE CENTRAL PROBLEM—THE EVEN PARTIAL ENUMERATION OF AN INFINITE WHOLE—HAS NO SOLUTION. "I FELT INFINITE REVERENCE, INFINITE PITY." "YOU MUST BE GAGA FROM ALL THAT POKING ABOUT WHERE YOU WEREN'T WANTED," SAID AN ODIOUS AND JOVIAL VOICE. "NO MATTER HOW YOU RACK YOUR BRAINS, YOU'LL NEVER REPAY MY REVELATION. THE PERFECT OBSERVATORY, EH, BORGES?"

It was customary at the stone chapel for one or another of the children to lead the Lord's Prayer during Mass. For a long time I wasn't allowed to do it, and when my turn came at last I nearly missed my cue. "Lizi! Viterbo! The Lord's Prayer!" came impatient whispers from all sides. At last I shouted a haughty "Our! Father!" to the altar, my voice ringing clearly and precisely in the silence like a bell or a song. My parents exchanged proud glances. But on the way home (we gave the congregation Sunday breakfast, cocoa and raisin cakes on tables set up in our garden) the chubby-cheeked priest came up to me and, all embarrassed and apologetic, said, *"You must keep calm, Lizi dear."* Then he put his hand on my head. *"You must look after yourself."* He was a good man, but I didn't care for his smell, a sickly-sweet combination of soap and sweat.

A queen, on the other hand, smells good. Just before the Battle of Budaörs Charles IV and Zita were held up for a while on a commercial track outside our garden. "Long live the eenquay!" I cried. Ostenburg, the aide-de-camp, took me up to Zita, who took me in her arms. But no matter.

<And the awful country waltz drones on and on.>

"WE SAID THAT IF YOU SHIT ON VÍZAKNA IT DOESN'T MEAN A THING, BUT IF VÍZAKNA SHITS ON YOU YOU'LL NEVER WASH IT OFF." AUNT RÓZA NODDED AND SAID, "TRUE." THEY'RE ONLY ANECDOTES, OF COURSE, BUT SCHOLARLY DISQUISITIONS WOULD BE EVERY BIT AS ANECDOTAL GIVEN THE CONTEXT. WORDS ARE ALL TOO TAME.

My stamping mysteriously called forth a mysterious underground cavern beneath the arborvitae, with crumbling steps leading to its depths. Yet elegant flowers blossomed amidst the mildew, rust, and rubble—gladioluses and orchids. There were a lot of tiny people milling about down there. It took me a long time to get my bearings. I was like the Emmaus disciples. I couldn't decide whether we were at a posh party or an ironworks. People were drinking elderberry wine from silver goblets.

They gave me a nice reception even though I was too big. The more we talked the better we got on. It was the first time I realized I could love people other than parents and siblings. They told me I was welcome whenever I pleased—all I had to do was stamp—but asked me not to tell anyone about them.

Still, I had to share my joy with Mother, and that evening I heard her and my poor father laughing over the "elaborate product" of their "Lizi's overactive fantasy life." I rushed out to the arborvitae to keep from hearing anything else they might say, and began scraping the shiny green moss with my nails. "I scrape you here, I scrape you there," I sobbed, thinking of my father. (Let me stress this was *not* a dream; it was my domain!)

There's a war on, I think, and everything is gray. The grayness is a substance. The garden wilts, shrinks, blackens as if burnt to a crisp, then starts melting-flowing-dripping like the *clocks* in a Dalí painting. And again time the miser is shrinking. The garden has turned into a desert. The whole family has to flee, though from what is not clear. Everything has a meaning: the wind blows, the sand shifts, my skirt sticks to my thighs, I drag my knapsack around like a humpbacked invalid, I have sand in my blouse. My first memory of my breasts is of *pouring sand out of the bra cups, weeping, but when I go to put the bra back on I have no breasts, nothing to hold up. . . .*

Then a monstrous balloon appears above me in the shape of my brother. He laughs, then tosses down a red pear at least two meters long. He waves, gives a cheerful shrug, and flies off. There I stand, all alone in that wasteland I could once call home. The pear has the shape of my breast.

MAY THIS YEW MERGE IMPERCEPTIBLY WITH YOUR GRACE'S GARDEN AS OUR SIGHS MERGE WITH THE FIRMAMENT. BOTH EASTWARDS AND WESTWARDS.

I put on a lot of weight when I was fourteen, though I was a good skier. I liked thick, heavy, flannel trousers; at first they rubbed against my thighs, but later I got used to them. The snow would burn, crunching and crackling like a campfire. Shoo, Miklós! We're putting out the fire! But Miklós didn't budge; he just said contemptuously, "*Let the gendarme burn in it!*" That sentence was like a human; I looked all over for it in the room the next morning. The hose coiled beautifully; it was a perfectly good hose, but those little sausages were inlaid with diamonds and real pearls. It may all have been a ruse to distract us from the dangerous fire! Well, it succeeded.

That was a time when I laughed at everything: myself, boys, girls, my mother, my father, kohlrabi, copper mortars, chicken soup, Ursa Major, my brother Miklós, the twisty-turny freight train, the hand that pockets the change, trouser legs, or rather all parts of trousers, especially flies and cuffs, the postman's stutter, a crooked stamp. I found everything irresistibly amusing. I laughed at the sea, dawn and dusk, silvery spiderwebs, the mirror, glances, clusters of grapes, bras, breast cancer, a stretch of broken-down fence, the Caspian Sea, the delicate bone structure of a hand, the incredibly explicit and obscene letters to a chorus girl from Debrecen left in a drawer of the rolltop desk (the handwriting made me shudder: the letters were written by my poor father); I laughed at my relatives' frightful remains and the circulation of my dark blood; I laughed at lovers entwined and death transmogrified.

I was merciless and kindhearted.

Ugly too, because my face had grown—its surface!—and bulged like a pillow. People didn't like me; I got on their nerves. I was prettier later, but nicer back then (though I wouldn't have said so at the time . . .).

DURING THE MEAL HE SAW HIS MOTHER ALL BUT REGURGITATE A PIECE OF BREAD, THEN HIDE IT IN HER HAND AND ROLL IT UP IN HER NAPKIN. "THANK YOU," HE SAID TETCHILY AT THE END OF THE MEAL, "BUT WHY MUST YOU BE SO SELF-SACRIFICING?" "THAT'S NOT FAIR OF YOU," THE WOMAN SAID WITH UNEXPECTED CLEMENCY, AND THEN ADDED, "I NEVER THOUGHT I'D SPEAK TO YOU ABOUT SUCH THINGS, MY BOY. IT'S UNHEALTHY TO BE THE MOTHER OF A GROWN MAN. A GOOD THING YOU'RE A BOY OR I'M A WOMAN. IT WOULD NOT HAVE BEEN EASY ON YOUR FATHER."

The arborvitaes have been torn out by the roots like molars, the fence pulled down, the kennels overturned, Mitzi the fawn's deep, crimson wound is swarming with flies, and the horses have broken loose. Anna bellows at the foreigners. I composed her love letters for her. "To Annuska Máli, radiant amongst roses," wrote her cavalier, and I answered, if . . . if she let Miklós lie at her side or, rather, *hide* his head between her breasts.

She shooed away the huge army trucks like stray animals. One of them rammed into the wall of a house, and although the driver jumped out in time he immediately started shrinking, as if the air had been let out of him, and vanished in the grass!

I set to looking for him at once, because he was such a good-looker; for starters, he had the same mustache as that nice Mikhalkov. But I kept coming up with a scaled-down copy of the pleasure-loving French governess. "That's some *bosom* you've got there, Mademoiselle Beatriz," she whispered contemptuously, the dried-out weed of a fool. (She may have been right, because the village children all called me Titty Lizi, though I wasn't ashamed of it for long.) I found her boring and crumbled her between my fingers. *Excusay-mwa. <Pieces for Player Piano!!!>*

I whiled away the hours walking around a beautiful castle. I was still chubby, but I'd stopped grinning all the time and I enjoyed dressing like a boy and going skating and horseback riding. I had a fur-lined coat from Transylvania, light as a feather, you know the kind. Now that it's gone, I freeze every winter.

I looked through the sumptuously mirrored rooms,

examined the faïence dishes, the Sèvres fireplaces, the clever patterns in the parquet floors. The Danube flowed from one room to the next, a meter or so wide. It stretched from the Black Forest to the Black Sea. The ceiling was decorated with frescoes. I stood on Great Schütt Island unloading reeds. The ceiling was light blue, like your friend's eyes. That was why I decided to use the castle for a charity exhibition of birds from the *entire* Danube region—and also, logically enough, because the Danube flows through it.

"Barbitum, barbitorium!" I roared, awakening with a start, my hair knotted with sweat. But no one could say what it meant. I was sitting on the peak of a large, majestic mountain with the sea stretching out before me and a cage of shame (on display in Lőcse) hanging over my head, and I was screaming in terror, "Barbitum, barbitorium!" I had a man's voice.

A boy put his arms around me; I came up to his shoulders. He was dripping concentrated sweat, but I didn't dare—or wish—to tell him. Nor could I decide whether the smell was a mistake. When he kissed me, I realized he had bad breath as well. That was the limit.

But until then we had been carried along by the crowd. The town crier told us, "I hereby inform you" that we were about to see Hungary's history, "the tearstained yet glorious pages of our orphaned homeland"—the Siege of Eger *straight ahead,* the Rout at Mohács *to the left,* the Cumin Invasion and Pecheneg Uprising *to the south,* and Genghis Khan's Great Offensive *to the right.* At last the boy dragged me to a small deserted square where we danced to wild *rock music.*

Completely unexpected. Trees and bushes—peeing! The sun beat down on the arch, the countryside was imbued with a golden glimmer, sheen, beauty, color—and the stink of urine!

I was young again. My brothers and sisters and I were getting ready for a party when Mama broke in on us in tears and *reported,* "My mother's passed away." Well, we were annoyed, because we still had work to do on our outfits and our grandmother had been an incapacitated, arterially scleroticized "somebody" for years. Mother sensed our annoyance, and her beautiful brown eyes swelled to apple size, popped out of their sockets, and drifted about the apartment gushing tears.

Still, my outfit was the most elegant. I danced with my nose in the air. "Whose hands is your future in?" I asked an extremely good-looking young man in my most aggressive manner. He smiled. "My own," he said, squeezing my face in his hot hands. "But my own are in God's." They had an honest-to-goodness orchestra. The boys went wild and stuffed corncobs in their slacks. I was forced to dance with my brother Bandi; his white suit gave off a delicate tobacco smell, but he tried to woo me like the others, so I had to run away. Guszti Kelemen was waiting outside in a dinghy, but your father was in it too and I couldn't tell if he was laughing or crying, only that he was laughing or crying. Guszti had lots of rubles. A ruble was as big as a fairly large towel. Guszti motioned to me under cover that I shouldn't say anything to your father about the money. He bought me an ugly-red, red-gold leather wallet in a floating boat shop. Then your father turned around—but I was young and he the age he is now, though still extremely good-looking—and said calmly, "Really, Lizi, what do you want with Guszti? . . . He has no taste. . . . *Why, that's artificial leather!*"

I forgot the rest, because I'm having an angiogram at the hospital tomorrow.

I entered a library the size of the one in Zirc, and there on a high-backed, Spanish Gothic chair sat the *Baron Uzuzor* in his usual threadbare blue-satin jodhpurs and jacket. He plied me with books—"My dear Elena, these are *einfach* indispensable to your spiritual development"—and always begged me to look at him, look him in the eye, and I was only too happy to. "It's so *marvelous,* Beatriz Elena my dear, it's in your eyes, infinity lurks in your eyes, that regal ferocity, you are capable of anything, you'll see, there will be great exultation, my child, your whole life, you still have a lot to learn, and I can tell that that's what makes you so trusting, but even so! you are marvelous, Beatriz, a free agent . . . you're . . . you're so daring, alluring, you *radiate!*" Then he sobbed and said, "O Miss Viterbo, how I should like to have two, at least two lives, so I could devote one entirely to you, it would be all yours, because I am not yours now and you are not mine, well, all right, I don't want to alarm you, with one of my two lives I'd forever be at your side. . . . I'd learn from you, from your cells, I'd watch your eyes, your mane. . . . I know you want nothing out of life, Miss Viterbo, *I'm* the one who wants something, you . . . but you want no . . . you want no sacrifice . . . because you, my dear, you are life itself!" But then the shiny, strong cherry-wood shelves disappeared in a flash and the books rose up the wall in a threatening jumble like a pile of chipped, mortar-splotched bricks. (Which reminds me of the time an old friend, Elemér Géczi, inquired rhetorically of himself, "Did the world come into being because of books?" to which he immediately replied, pointing to the piles of books in his room, "Not in the slightest." "Why not tidy up a bit?" "It makes no sense, Lizi, not for so short a time." And so he said for twenty years running. He died in '45, starved to death, like Dezső Szabó. You know his daughter. She has black hair, sometimes wears it in a bun. A bitch, if you want to know the truth. God, the tricks she tried with your father! But for some reason he didn't see anything in her. "Fool that I am, Lizi, I've never once deceived you." Well, actually I know the reason: S. was in love with me, but she would have been satisfied with your father.) The library was practically drizzling dust, and we stood knee deep in tormented books. All at once in stepped an incredibly slovenly woman and announced that dinner was served. The moment she saw me, she started shaking the Baron. "Grab me, you fool! Hug me! Fling me to the ground! . . . What more do you need? Inhale me like a cigarette, squeeze me till I crack, hack me to pieces! Can't you be more human! . . . No, you're ridiculous!" The Baron, never one for self-control, shoved the evil-tongued woman out of the room, screaming, "You call those *breasts?!* They're no breasts! They're sausage ends!" I can still hear his hoarse, agitated, furious voice screaming, They're no breasts! They're sausage ends!

IT'S NOT TRUE THAT WRITING HAS HELPED ME. DURING THE WEEKS I WORKED ON THE STORY THE STORY NEVER CEASED TO WORK ON ME. WRITING HAS NOT BEEN, AS I SUPPOSED AT FIRST, THE REMEMBERING OF A SET PERIOD IN MY LIFE BUT ONLY A CONSTANT AFFECTATION OF REMEMBERING IN THE FORM OF SENTENCES THAT MERELY CLAIM DETACHMENT. EVEN NOW I WAKE UP IN THE NIGHT WITH A START, NUDGED OUT OF SLEEP BY SOME-

THING WITHIN ME, AND, BREATHLESS WITH HORROR, FEEL MYSELF DECOMPOSING FROM ONE SECOND TO THE NEXT. THE AIR IN THE DARKNESS IS SO STILL THAT THINGS SEEM TO HAVE LOST THEIR EQUILIBRIUM, BE TORN FROM THEIR MOORINGS, AND ONCE THEY'VE FLOATED NOISELESSLY ABOUT FOR A WHILE WITH NO CENTER OF GRAVITY THEY SUDDENLY COME CRASHING DOWN ON ALL SIDES AND SMOTHER ME. THESE ANXIETY ATTACKS MAKE ME AS MAGNETIC AS ROTTING CARRION, AND WHAT I EXPERIENCE IN PLACE OF AN INDIFFERENT SENSE OF WELL-BEING, WHERE FEELINGS FREELY INTERACT WITH ONE ANOTHER, IS INDIFFERENT, OBJECTIVE TERROR.

I married Guszti Kelemen. Your father just looked on. He was mortally offended. I thought I had made the right decision. It was a scorching summer. I walked down to the Danube on a royal purple carpet of soft asphalt and played "ducks and drakes," but I could never get a stone to skip more than thirteen times, because something always snapped it up. I went after it and pulled a gigantic green snake out of the water.

I dragged this ravishing and repellent bridal veil through the streets, constantly sinking into the asphalt. "What in the world are you doing, Miss Lizi?" the butcher called out. The bus drivers swerved around me with a curse. And I didn't even know whether the snake was poisonous. At last I dragged it into the kitchen, chopped its head off, sliced it into cutlets, and roasted it. "Beef Wellington! And better than Wellington ever ate!" Well, I'm the best judge of that. I can never remember what *origano* means.

I went to see the Sistine Chapel. I saw scaffolding and boxes of mortar and empty beer bottles with KINIZSI labels—you'd think the stonemasons were Hungarian—and I climbed all the way up to the ceiling and lay down as Michelangelo did when he painted. *Everything* was so close that I took the Lord's outstretched hand. Nothing too awful can happen anymore, I thought. Then I clambered down quickly and ran off to the Vatican. Purple-cinctured priests opened the white double doors for me with deep, reverent bows as if I were Miklós Szentkuthy stark naked, and I heard my name come buzzing down from all sides, Beatriz, Beatriz Elena, Beatriz Elena Viterbo, O my darling Beatriz . . .

At last I kneeled before the Holy Father and, still panting from my run, asked him for some chocolate. "With nuts, please, Holy Father!" You will understand it all better if I tell you that whereas my father was a Calvinist, Mama was Catholic, so I had every right to the nuts. I should also note that I was present at Pope Paul VI's funeral. I wore a black mantle and a white porcelain chamber pot. After it was over, I chose the new pope.

IT IS TIME FOR ME TO REIN IN MY INSPIRATION AND PAUSE A MOMENT ON MY WAY LIKE A MAN PEERING INTO A WOMAN'S VAGINA. IT IS FITTING FOR ME TO LOOK BACK OVER THE ROAD COVERED AND THEN, LIMBS RESTORED, LEAP UP AND SPEED OFF.

Your father sat night after night with my parents picking apart Guszti Kelemen. He may have been dead by then. Somebody wrote to me later that he caught dysentery on the Don or something. We lived together for three weeks, three weeks. He was the first man in my life. You don't expect me to forget that, do you? . . . Your father is my lord and master, but I can't help trembling at the thought of the man to whom I surrendered my virginity.

They would talk in the dining room over dirty dishes. Leftovers! I stalked them in my socks and black apron, the one with the large pockets I kept a skeleton key in. Clever little gadget. I was not an easy child. Next to the kitchen we had a pantry that wasn't a closet but a real *room,* a larder!, where all sorts of edible wonders lay hidden. I would break in with my skeleton key and wrap up pastries in tissue paper—they had chocolate icing on top and were all sticky. Then I'd dig into the raisin box—a large, fragrant mahogany chest with hinges as big as fists—and sprinkle my booty on the icing! I was also known to have stuck a homemade salami under my skirt. Then I'd run out to the fence, where my little peasants were waiting, and—don't miss this, my boy, a bit of social activism for you (we can put it in the inventory)—hand out the treasures. It made them happy, and they gave me good black bread in exchange, which made *me* happy.

Meanwhile, back in the house they were saying nasty things about my life. Your father got on well with my parents; he was a nice boy—polite, accommodating, and witty. Your father was as elegant as Abbazia. My mother wore a beige tunic-like dress. It had

a light brown silk fringe along the bottom—I'm sure of it.

DON'T FORGET YOU'RE A LOVE CHILD.
DON'T BE SILLY! WHO ISN'T?

We were young. Or, rather, I was young in years, because I was already your father's wife. And did I give him a hard time! I'd disappear for days on end. The music stopped for a while, and we girls went out for a breath of air and a chance to get away from the boys and talk over our relations with them, the results of our betrayals and defeats, but suddenly we were in the courtyard of a filthy tenement house with tumbledown galleries, the kind you see in socially aware photography of the thirties. I was walking around a sumac tree with Ágnes Záhy when Blanka suddenly yelled down to us—God, she was young and beautiful, elegant and stylish—cursing like a trooper. When she finished and disappeared, Ágnes planted herself in front of me and started picking the flowers off her pink evening gown and pelting me with them: I had told her in the dance hall that so many flowers were both unflattering to her and inappropriate to the occasion.

The flowers came to life as she removed them, and I lay in a fragrant flower grove. Your father saw me home and took good care of me, never saying anything nasty or even harboring nasty thoughts, which is why I loved him so. (I was wrong to let him call me Lizi; horses called me Lizi. [?])

Vali Dienes, who was my grandmother's cousin and who taught me orchestics when I was just starting Gymnasium, came in the door in my dream and observed in her beautiful, deep voice that we had better take the liver pâté out of the icebox—it had *gone bad*—and give it to the dog. "Liver pâté is no joke, Lizi darling," she said. The next morning, though I didn't see anything suspicious about it, I told your father to throw out the liver pâté. First he spread some on a slice of bread (which was just like him: he'd have felt bad about chucking the whole thing) and then grumbling (he was a grumbler!) threw it away.

Aunt Vali was wearing a long black shroud, which she wore in life as well. She always had a few meters of material wound round her. She died at the age of ninety-nine. She was a disciple of Bergson, I believe. A pity you didn't know her, my son.

I RESOLVED TO LIVE FREE, AS MEN DO—STRONG, INDEPENDENT, IN THE WIND—BUT WITHOUT ASCRIBING ANY SIGNIFICANCE TO IT. I WOULD ACCEPT ALL LIFE'S GIFTS—THE FINE THINGS IT HAD TO OFFER AND ITS BAD JOKES—AS WHAT I HAD COMING TO ME. I WOULD BE MY OWN MISTRESS, I DECIDED, THE HEROINE OF MY OWN LIFE.

Your father was always very nice with the help. He could afford to be. I was in an alien atmosphere and much more haughty. "Watch out you don't get drenched, Fräulein Käthe!" "Don't worry, sir! Most of it is falling off to the side." The rain was coming down in buckets; the horses were standing there resigned. At the farmhouse your father put his hand on mine, and because I didn't want a scandal I pinched his calf when nobody was looking. All he did was laugh. "You whistle like a peasant, you wonderful woman, you!" That was long ago.

In the morning I went out into the garden. A large, green rectangle. The sun was shining, the grass soaking wet. I lay down in the hammock. There is a scrap of felt at the point of suspension: we are tree-lovers. *Frühlingsbad.*

Young girls come up to my swinging bed in high-necked blouses, but their flared skirts fairly swirl. "Excuse us, miss," they say with sheepish smiles, "but the water is boiling in the vats out in the laundry, and we've scoured the tub, scoured the tub. The hoops that bind the boards are the size of the mistress's hips, and the tiny windows are coated with steam. Your *Frühlingsbad* is ready, miss!" I twist my head to the side; the sun is a large ball, the rectangle pure green.

I see him on the terrace. His pajamas are half open to let in the sunlight. There's nothing new about this kind of flirtation in men, not for me, at least. There he stands, as limp and lazy as I might stand there. Revolting. I bawl him out. The scorching sun—I see it! I see it!—gives him confidence, and he gives a barely visible shrug. A shudder runs through the pajamas.

"Why is Aachen Cathedral like a hare, Beatriz darling? Let me tell you. Aachen Cathedral is like a hare because if you don't approach it with great caution and a pure heart it will make tracks." That is what he called humor. "Your caresses were so false today, darling, that I pitied you."

OFTEN WHILE WORKING ON THE STORY I FELT THAT THE EVENTS WOULD BE BETTER SERVED IF THEY WERE SET TO MUSIC. SWEET NEW ENGLAND . . .

I went around Budapest in men's clothing. And at night. I was tired and ugly. I didn't meet a soul. The city was empty. Then I spied a soldier. At last, an *adventure!* I thought, an adventure; I'll look him straight in the eye. He was young, sleepy, and dejected, but I could see he liked me. He said he would show me around. He dragged me through the dead stone colossi to all the heroic monuments. Every last one of them! The whole night. *I know all your monuments like the back of my hand!*

In the fuzzy zone between night and dawn he proposed we piss together. Soldiers and piss are inseparable. Too late, I thought, you can't seduce me now. I'm *like a bored-open poppyhead.* I dreamed the simile too.

"Now I'm going to buy you a drink," he said grandly. We landed in a rock-bottom dive. All soldiers. No hookers even. "My treat," he said, as touching as before. He ordered lemonade—*pink* (!) lemonade—and hard-boiled eggs.

At that point the scales fell from my eyes, and I realized he was your father begging me not to make a scandal and casting sidelong glances at "the distinguished officers of the people's democracy." "Beatriz, my dearest, it's time to go."

"I'll eat my egg even if you burst."

But then I lost weight, just for fun, because though I'd always carried around what is commonly called a bit of extra baggage I sort of liked it and I knew other people liked it, everybody likes it. I spent ten days taking saunas and doing calisthenics; I ate five or six hard-boiled eggs a day. . . . I was very proud of how loosely my slacks hung on me.

After that I found myself mentally encouraging men in the tram to notice my new beauty and screw up the courage to stroke my face, which had now lost its ugly pouches, while my shoulders remained "regal" and there was no longer any need to keep a certain fleshy quality of the back a guilty secret, and so on, and I mentally haggled over myself, driving the price higher and higher. . . .

EVERYONE HERE, MYSELF INCLUDED, IS SO DISGUSTINGLY NORMAL.

Let me tell you a story. It will do you good. Once upon a time your father put on long raven wings. "What are you doing?" I asked him, amazed. "I am putting on long raven wings." "Well, you listen to me, my pet: if I catch you putting on long raven wings again, I won't answer for my actions." Then we ran down to catch the number 4 tram, because we didn't want to miss our early morning indoctrination sessions, and we lived happily ever after.

I don't feel those feelings, my son; all I can think of are words of humiliation. But when it comes to words, that's how it is. "Why do you put so much faith in words, Lizi?" your father once asked me. "What should I put faith in, silly? You?! God forbid!"

We used to go on picnics all the time; I'd carry the food in a wicker basket, and he'd bring a bottle of wine, "a light distillation of homegrown juniper berries," which he swung like a doll. We'd go up in the mountains. I can't believe I didn't sleep with him.

Years later, after an awful fight, your father mounted me, bone-drunk, and I didn't brush him off (like a caterpillar—I say caterpillar, perhaps, because the stomach he pressed to mine was white and cold), I was afraid, we had nasty quarrels, too fast, and I was sorry too, disgusted but sorry for us, and lay there stiff, my legs spread, "Help me, damn it!" he panted, and I shut my eyes so as not to see his face, but I could see and feel everything behind my eyelids. "No, no, you, no! Damn!" But before the night was over he'd sobered up (halfway), poor thing, and he began to tell me (!) how much he'd wanted me that time in the woods, but I hadn't even resisted him, because I didn't grasp his private, vibrating currents—no wonder he felt so *helpless* sometimes. . . . The idiot! If he had known how I came home from the picnic, all feverish and tearful, and brushed past my mother . . . and well, if he had known how much I loved him when I loved him.

"DO YOU LOVE ME OR ARE YOU JUST PLAYING AN UGLY GAME?" WHINE! THERE'S MY FATHER'S BED. IN IT, MY FATHER. ATTITUDE OF DEJECTION. GRACEFUL AS A MULE DEER ONCE, THE SAME LARGE EARS. FOR A NANOSECOND THERE IS A NANOSMILE. IS HE HAVING ME ON? I REMEMBER ONCE WE WENT OUT ON THE UPS AND DOWNS OF THE WEST (OUT PAST VULTURE'S ROOST) TO SHOOT. . . . IT WAS PRETTY BORING SHOOTING UP MESQUITE BUSHES, SO WE HUNKERED DOWN BEHIND SOME ROCKS, FATHER AND I, HE HUNKERED DOWN BEHIND HIS ROCK AND I HUNKERED DOWN BEHIND MY ROCK, AND WE COMMENCED TO SHOOTING AT EACH OTHER. THAT WAS INTERESTING.

I was as old as I am now when I first hijacked a plane. Where to is of no interest. I asked the sexy pilot to intercede with the authorities on my behalf so we could keep the affair under wraps. The press passed over it in silence. You can check if you like, my son.

Rembrandt has a painting called *Ganymede in the Eagle's Claws*. One night I soared up into the heights and saw the little naked boy peeing. I flew over to him, but the eagle bit me in the arm. It had eyes full of hate. So I swooped down, and Ganymede waved to me. . . .

I have no desire to see the other world. On principle, I mean. I don't think God wants us to. I don't mean to hurt your feelings; I don't write "your God." I have no trouble with God; I don't hate Him for not existing.

There are times when I forget I'm alive. I sit amidst a stack of pillows and talk to God. He's like *Vili Tátray* without the violin. But whenever I sit on the stool and watch the fluff under the bed try to roll over the chaff, I realize—and occasionally even feel—I'm alive. Well, enough of that. I also wanted to let you know I had a nosebleed in the garden. I'd dragged the garden chair over to the sand pit, and that's where it happened. The sand went all black from the blood. I let my head hang down and the blood drip out; I didn't dare lean backwards the way they say you should, because I was afraid of choking to death like our King Attila. Reaching up to my nose and scratching away the splotches of dried blood was so *foreign* to me that I shuddered, positively shuddered.

What makes me happiest of all is that I can sleep alone.

Lying in my bed by myself, my hands behind my neck, I think of you, my son.

IF PEOPLE COULD CHOOSE WHOM TO RESURRECT, DO YOU THINK THEY'D CHOOSE JESUS?

On the eve of your funeral, my son, I'll arrive from a great distance. I'll be tired, and my blouse will be drenched with sweat. I'll find a place to bathe and rinse off the road's gray dust. Having nothing to wear, I'll ask my sister's assistance. I'll be annoyed that her clothes become me, but glad when I see in her eyes that I am beautiful.

I'll embrace her; she'll be surprised.

"Have some, Lizi," she'll say, proffering a platter of crackling cakes. (She has a reputation for crackling cakes. I look down on her because she uses a scale when she cooks. I estimate.) That's when I'll burst into tears. "Have some, Lizi, it will calm your nerves." My hand will contract in a spasm, the cake crumble through my fingers, and I'll say, "I don't want to be calm, for God's sake. What is there to be calm about?" and I'll weep and weep. And my beautiful idiotic sister will hug me and *comfort* me, which will only make me laugh through my tears.

Swaying, leaning on each other, we'll waltz around the room. Down come the crackling cakes from their silver platter, plip plop, and your uncle, an official *amoroso* of sorts, will pick them up from the floor with a smile.

I won't cry again until your name is sponged off the mortuary slate, my son, and you're no longer *next.*

I WILL ERASE, ELIMINATE ALL SIGNS. I WILL USE FORCE OR CUNNING TO RETRIEVE AND DESTROY ALL THE DEATH NOTICES DISPATCHED BY POST. I WILL PROCEED SIMILARLY WITH ALL COPIES OF THE ISSUE OF *MAGYAR NEMZET* IN WHICH THE ANALOGOUS ANNOUNCEMENT

APPEARED. I WILL, BY MEANS OF SLOW AND CAREFUL RUBBING, REMOVE FROM THE GRAVESTONE ALL TRACES OF—IN THE FOLLOWING ORDER—MY MOTHER'S NAME, HER TWO DATES, AND FINALLY THE CROSS, AND I SOLEMNLY VOW TO SIN NO MORE.

What will your funeral be like, my son? *Description:* You will have a stately military funeral with an honor guard of handsome youths, each of whom will have a small, delicate cut on his neck spurting black, viscous blood. But no matter. Then they'll tell the usual lies about the fatherland. The whole thing will be telecast in color. I'll turn off the sound while they shovel in the earth.

Description: At your funeral, my son, there will be speeches by fine, high-ranking, *hochintelligent* military men. Their manners will be elegant, and each of them will show at least a flash of deep, tragic wisdom. Each of them will have exquisite marbles for eyes. *Einstand.* But no matter. They'll tell their stale lies about the fatherland, but we'll be truly and deeply touched.

Description: The women will come to your funeral in bloodstained cambric. "It's starting," they'll whisper to one another, lowering their eyes when they see you. "Don't be annoyed, sir. I've got the curse." They will all kiss you on the mouth, the sluts. But no matter. The sight of your face repels me. Your lips are blue. Impossible!

Description: You're repulsive, my son, hateful, outlandish, enormous. How can I live without you? Why are you meddling in my life? But no matter. My words rain down upon me as the earth will rain down upon you. My eyes. My mouth.

Description: At your funeral, my son, I'll wait pensively while the gravediggers make a professional-looking

mound, and then with heavy heart and grotesque inepti-
tude I'll tumble headfirst like a clown into the clayey mud. Through half-closed eyelids I'll see my sister's humiliating sneer as she dries off my face, but I'll lie there among the ribbons, the silk ribbons coiling round me in profusion, and though the blockheads have left behind a wire wreath frame and it's killing me, I'll go on lying there, stretched out beside you, your swooning mother of the clay kiss. . . . I'll have trouble breathing. Gradually I'll come to believe my own bad joke. My sister knows all, I can see that.

GET A MOVE ON, COLORADO. TIME TO ROUSE THAT GUY IN THE COFFIN.

Description: At your funeral, my son, I'll cause a great scandal. I'll stop the shoveling and ask them to weigh each clod of earth. "To the gram!" I'll say to the silence in a tone that brooks no rebuff. My sister will take a shiny copper apothecary scale from her purse. "Why, of course," I'll say contemptuously. My sister is pretty and will smile and say, "I haven't got the weights." "Who has?" I'll ask, both shy and stern. The mourners will start whispering behind their hands, my son.

Description: At your funeral, my son, I'll accept condolences. When Blanka's turn comes, I'll give her a big hug. Mourning has disfigured her face: her forehead's too narrow, *everything's out of proportion,* her eyes have moved unintellectually close, and the fact that they're crossed doesn't help matters any. We'll be standing here a long time, and I'll shiver. My eyes will be open; I'll see the gravediggers leaning against a distant mound eating bacon. "Hey, Lajoska," I'll hear, "I got onions." I'm grateful, but no matter.

Description: At your funeral, my son, I want to be beautiful. Beautiful! Later I want to be an attractive, fragile woman, racked but not broken by grief, just strong enough so when people whisper behind my back they say, "What a beautiful woman," instead of "What a strong woman."

In the morning I'll stand in front of the mirror in my bra and practice shaking hands. Shall I say "Thank you" or "Yes"? I feel more comfortable with the latter. My deepest condolences. Yes. And how beautiful I'll be. *Black* will make me so desirable. *I shall be the earth,* I'll think, and men will enter me like worms. But no matter. I don't hate anyone.

"Pull yourself together, will you?" says my sister, none too softly.

Description: There will be a moment when I don't dare look at Blanka. I'll give her a big hug, clumsily seeking out her place with my thighs, and through my tears I'll see the gravediggers eating their bacon. Blanka will squeeze me, and I'll whisper, "I'm alive," to her, "I *am* alive, aren't I?" She has pierced ears. "Everything's fine, darling, everything's fine," she says, "couldn't be worse," and I repeat, "I *am* alive, aren't I?" almost triumphantly.

I want to be less conscious, my son. When I stand at your grave, I should be dumber than any animal; I shouldn't even think in sentences. When I stand at your grave, I should be: like you.

GET A MOVE ON, COLORADO. TIME TO ROUSE THAT GUY IN THE COFFIN.

Description: At your funeral, my son, I won't be able to take my aged eyes off you. There can be no friendship between mother and son. The son will immediately see the spy lurking behind the friend and the jealous woman behind the spy's back. You thought the two of us could be friends. . . . I ask your God to resurrect you. I'll offer him good terms. "Hear, O Lord, I'm off to a shrewd start."

Description: At your funeral, my son, the coffin will be spread with the Hungarian flag. Red! White! Green! But no matter. Then they'll tell the usual lies about the fatherland. I can hear your voice. "I've got the weights in my pocket," you'll giggle. But your friend the skinny priest will call for order. "*Attention, everyone,*" he'll say, and raise his hand. That's about all he can do. The thing I dislike about your God is His almightiness. . . . I think I'd feel better about it all if your friend over there wiping his steamed-up wire-rimmed glasses—if *he* were God. But no matter.

Description: There's a big problem, my son. Whether your God exists or not, this is no way to live. I beg you, my son—it's in your power—forgive me.

Description: I have described it: I will describe it. <I have described it.>

My son.

It's night now. Everything is foreign here. I can't even recognize the cars by their sound. I've been looking at

your picture and wondering whether there's an after-world and you still exist in some fashion, though the *molecules* will never come together as . . . I'm tired. I don't understand my loss; I accept it.

GET A MOVE ON, COLORADO. TIME TO ROUSE THAT GUY IN THE COFFIN.

I keep trying to tell myself you're dead, so I don't forget it for a moment, it would be painful, youaredeadyouare-deadyouaredead.

"Am I that heavy?" Mother asked as if she were scolding me.

I HADN'T SEEN MY FATHER FOR A LONG TIME, BUT IN LATE OCTOBER HE PHONED. HE WAS EXTREMELY AGITATED; I COULDN'T IDENTIFY HIS VOICE AT FIRST. SADLY AND ANGRILY HE STAMMERED OUT THAT THE UNBRIDLED ZUNINO AND ZUNGRI WERE GOING TO TEAR DOWN HIS HOUSE UNDER THE PRETEXT OF ENLARGING THEIR ALREADY ENORMOUS CONFECTIONER'S SHOP.

"THE HOUSE OF MY FATHERS, MY HOUSE, THE GOOD OLD CALLE GARAY HOUSE," HE KEPT SAYING, PERHAPS FORGETTING HIS SORROW IN THE MELODY OF IT.

I HAD NO DIFFICULTY SHARING HIS GRIEF. ONCE YOU'RE OVER THIRTY, EVERY CHANGE IS A LOATHSOME SYMBOL OF THE PASSAGE OF TIME. BESIDES, FOR ME THE HOUSE WAS AN ENDLESS ALLUSION TO BEATRIZ. I WISHED TO CLARIFY THIS HIGHLY DELICATE POINT, BUT MY CONVERSATION PARTNER DID NOT HEAR ME.

MY FATHER'S MISFORTUNE FILLED ME WITH MALICIOUS JOY. WE HAD ALWAYS HATED EACH OTHER IN PRIVATE.

THE SERVANT GIRL AT THE CALLE GARAY HOUSE—WHOM I HAD NEVER SEEN BEFORE AND WHO HAD, TO MY KNOWLEDGE, NEVER SEEN ME—ASKED IF I WOULD BE KIND ENOUGH TO WAIT. AS ALWAYS THE MASTER WAS IN THE BASEMENT DEVELOPING PICTURES. NEXT TO THE FLOWERLESS FLOWERPOT ON THE USELESS PIANO THE LARGE INEPTLY PIGMENTED PORTRAIT OF BEATRIZ SMILED AT ME (MORE TIMELESS THAN ANACHRONISTIC). NO ONE COULD SEE US. IN MY TENDER DESPAIR I WENT UP TO THE PORTRAIT AND SAID TO IT, "BEATRIZ, BEATRIZ

ELENA, BEATRIZ ELENA VITERBO, O MY DARLING BEATRIZ, THOU ART LOST AND GONE FOREVER, BUT I HAVE COME <CORRUPT TEXT>.

She is sitting in bed, propped up on pillows and observing my discomfort with a mildly condescending smile. A pale woman in a small room.

"Hand me the soup." A grayish brew sloshes in her cup. I watch the coagulated fat break loose from the porcelain wall. I find the slurping distasteful. The noodles dangle from her mouth. She sucks them in; they disappear with inordinate speed.

"How brave you are today," she says, still spooning it in. I leap up, more nimble than nettled. "Why don't you say something?" "I was about to," she answers, lowering her eyes. She's spilt her soup; a few thin noodle-bugs slide down her neck and wind up in the pale, liver-spotted hollow near the collarbone. I reach out; the noodles start disintegrating at my touch, but I manage to get them back into her cup one by one. Mother goes on eating unperturbed. A noodle slips down between her large, flat, white breasts. I reach for it; it divides in my fingers like a worm. I leave the lower half to continue on its way, and lift the half that remains and drop it in the saucer. "Last night I fell on my face," she says with a smile. "I rang three times!" By now she is laughing. "And in the end I wet the bed." I can smell it.

"Good, very good," she says, putting down her cup. "You've done a good job of feeding your aged mother." I take her hand. We sit for a long time in silence. I stare at the blanket.

"Let's go to the toilet," she says all of a sudden.

"Fine," I say, but I don't move, because I don't know what to do next.

"Stand up, put your hands under my arms, and lift me. Link your arm in mine. And keep an eye on my legs. Let's

go." Like a soldier or a consultant on an assignment, not bored but without the slightest sign of agitation.
OF COURSE, SOMETIMES WHILE WORKING ON THE STORY I GOT TIRED OF ALL THE FRANKNESS AND HONESTY AND LONGED TO GO BACK TO SOMETHING THAT WOULD GIVE ME A CHANCE TO LIE AND DISSEMBLE A BIT AS, SAY, USUAL.

I stand up. She leans forward and throws back the covers, a threadbare quilt and thin brown blanket with a large hole burnt into one edge. The perimeter of the hole is frayed and dark brown. She gasps in pain.

"Ouch!"

"Take it easy."

Her thin nightgown slips forward, and a stale odor escapes from the open bed. Now the nightgown slides up to the groin, and I give serious thought to whether I should acknowledge it. But it is so hard to accept that all this is real and happening to us at a given moment that (without meaning to brag) I push it out of my mind. The end of her pubic hair peeks out as if it didn't belong anywhere. The bandage goes from the base of her thighs to her knees. The skin around it is a yellowish brown, from the iodine perhaps. Her thighs and legs are very thin, her knees mere bony protuberances. Yet the legs still show their former beauty. The thighs don't meet; the flesh just hangs there. I touch her calves.

"They're nice and warm."

"They hurt. The blood is rushing through me—that's why."

One of her toenails is bruised and black, the others are yellowish. The toes are all callused. Moaning softly, she lowers one foot to the floor and feels around for her soft slipper. I look on motionless.

"Where are my nice soft slippers?" she asks in a hoarse voice. I push them over to her. "Be careful not to touch me."

"I am careful. You don't need to keep telling me."

She steadies herself with both hands; the bedsprings creak. Then she turns to let down the other leg, the bandaged one. All this wears her out, and she perches for a while on the edge of the bed, a ruffled sparrow. I adjust her thin, dirty, rumpled nightgown.

"Lift me by the armpits."

I brace myself, place my legs between hers, and lean over, trying to find a grip. That poor flesh! Her hair has an oily sheen; she smells stale. I make a face. The hair has parted in the middle and hangs down on both sides, leaving the ears free. In the shiny white space on the top of the head I see flakes of skin, tiny pale chips with strands of hair sticking through them.

ACCEPT OUR THANKS, O LORD, FOR THY DEVOTED FREUDLINESS.

My knees buckle as I take hold of her; our faces fall together as in a film.

"You've lost weight."

Her eyes seem to be lying at the bottom of a pit, they have black shadows around them; her cheeks are, as always, fat and round; both ends of her mouth show deep wrinkles and a few long hairs; her double chin looks funny now that it's shrunk—like a balloon with the air let out, it just hangs there.

Lifting her is easier than I thought; she moans softly, in pain, and her strong body odor hits me again.

"We're like a couple of lovers," she says in a detached voice.

I'm getting jittery. "Let's go."

"Give me your arm."

I give her my arm.

"Not like that," she says nervously. "Firmer." I must look too noble, too courteous or solicitous, because she adds, "We're not going on a promenade; we're going to the toilet."

We shuffle down the corridor, down the middle, to avoid the legs of the patients lounging along the walls. There are a number of them, some on the floor. It's dark. Here and there a crutch rises in the air. The toilet is at the end of the corridor, a long way off. She stops to rest. I lean on her. I don't know where to look; I don't want to look at her. Despite the noise from the twisting pipes and the constant murmur of the patients, all I can hear is her wheezing.

One of the crutches, tripped by a stone slab that isn't flush with the rest, slides down the wall with a great crash. I step over it, but Mother pauses: all she can do is shuffle. I can't let her go, so I look around to see who the crutch belongs to. Its position seems to indicate a body swathed in rags and topped with blood-soiled gauze and the crown of a head. I say something to it, but to no avail: the head does not flinch. I try again, more than once. Finally, a thin, hysterical voice emerges from the enormous, rustic body of an old woman sitting on a suitcase (her face is full, she looks strong all over, what's she doing here?): "Are you an idiot? A complete idiot? Can't you see he's dead?"

WHAT DO YOU WANT? CAN'T YOU SEE I'M DIGGING A GRAVE? A FEEDING LION WILL NOT TOLERATE INTRUSION. IF YOU DON'T KNOW THAT, I'LL TEACH YOU. COME ALONG NOW, GO TO, DO WHAT YOU'VE ALWAYS WANTED TO.

Almost by way of retaliation I give the crutch a kick, but it gets caught in my shoe and swirls like a happy-go-lucky walking stick. The coast is clear. Nobody says a word. I should have done it immediately.

"I didn't know you had it in you."

I shrug.

When we get to the door of the toilet, I hesitate for a moment.

"Come on. You think I'll be able to make it on my own from here?"

The men's toilet is nailed shut, so we shuffle off to the women's. Mother grabs hold of the wooden partition. The first stall is empty but out of paper; I dig in under the lid to make sure.

"I've brought some with me," she says, taking it out of her nightgown.

"Where in the world do you keep it?"

"I've sewn a little pocket in. A secret pocket."

I automatically look over as she reaches down to a space between the last two buttons. I peer into the opening. Again I see that the top part of her pubic hair has been shaved off. I'm moved. So that's it! *They've trimmed the dwarf's beard.* Stubble. I feel like running the balls of my fingers over the cut hair's bristly base.

"It was a mistake, the idiots! You know what they said? That they thought I was here to give birth."

"And weren't they a bit *suspicious* when they saw you had no stomach?"

"Maybe I was fatter then."

"Don't be silly," I say without thinking, and blush, all of which riles her even more. I don't react.

We shuffle into the stall. All she cares about now is

doing her business. She lifts her nightgown and spreads her legs. I take her by the armpits to ease her down.

"No," she says. "Put paper on the seat first." And she reaches into her secret pocket, thereby letting go of the crumpled nightgown, which drops in a white flash and so suddenly that we each make a dive for it, she begins to totter, I reach out for her, I lose my balance and grab her waist with one hand and steady myself against the wall behind the toilet with the other. The plaster flakes.

GRIEF AND INFINITY. THIN-FLANKED DOGS WITH RIBS OF WOVEN TWIGS SPEED PAST NOISELESSLY. CROWS TAKE FLIGHT IN THE WHITE WOUNDS OF THE LANDSCAPE. OF COURSE, OF COURSE, FORGETTING, TIME PAST. BUT WHERE DID I LEAVE OFF? AM I REALLY ALIVE? IT'S REALLY HARD, MOTHER. REALLY HARD.

"What are you doing, silly?"

"Holding on."

I lean over the toilet, but she bends back, into my arms, almost as if we were dancing. The trouble is I can't move to the side because I'm standing between her legs. My arms are getting tired. I decide to put all my weight on the pipe leading down from the flush box, and after a moment of uncertainty we're on firm ground again.

"Where did we leave off?"

"The paper," she answers, grabbing my neck and reaching into her inner pocket.

I yield to the balls of my fingers.

"I'm freezing."

"Yes."

Her backside is all goose pimples, her flesh thin and cold.

"What are you waiting for, for God's sake!" She bursts into dry tears. "I've got to sh . . . !"

"All right, all right," I mutter in a panic. "You can sit down now."

"The paper," she says, and doesn't budge. She is holding on to my neck and feels strong again. "My breath smells of medicine," she adds.

I don't notice; I am trying to spread the paper over the toilet seat. I go easy on it because I consider it entirely unnecessary. At last I put my hands back under her arms. "There, you can sit down now."

She lifts her nightgown and shuffles a bit, trying to find her footing. I start letting her down; her knees bend. The position clearly puts me at her mercy; I flash a glance at the pipe. The paint is blistering. Mother groans.

"I can't. My legs won't bend." We stand there. She is

the practical one. "But I only need to pee anyway." I don't move: once more I don't know what to do. "Lean over, darling, and lift the seat." I immediately think of the paper and retrieve it, as I laid it out, with much scuffing of feet. I stick it in the pocket of my jeans. "Don't forget to give it back," she admonishes me seriously.

I pick up the seat, and she pees in an upright position with a good deal of splashing. I start laughing and she joins in, whereupon the splish-splash breaks off. "Be serious. How can I pee if I'm laughing?" And although a few more drops emerge, she's annoyed. "Why did you bother me like that? Now it's stuck in there."

SHE TOOK HER SECRET TO THE GRAVE.

We start back, shuffling our woebegone way down the corridor, the crutch still where I kicked it, the peasant woman where we left her—I look at her, she looks me up and down self-confidently, and on we go.

"Tired?"

A scornful wave of the hand tells me that my eager-beaver tact gets on her nerves—I'm not surprised—and I put her in bed, clear a chair, and sit down next to her.

"Oh, how warm the bed is," she sighs. I sit there, stroking her hand, her rough, scaly hand. She falls asleep. . . . I carefully slide my hand from under hers and slip off towards the door, as if she were still by my side.

"Don't go."

I turn. Her face has disappeared in the puffed-up pillow; her face is red, her eyes sparkle from the depths of the pit. We look at each other. — — — — She makes a place for me, and I lie down in the troughlike hollow her body has carved out. I turn on my side and let my shoes hang off the bed. She turns to me impetuously; I can feel she has a fever. She is crying again. We stay like that.

"You!"

"Yes?"

"You!"

I say "You!" back.

"You!" she says playfully, making believe she's embarrassed. "You . . . give me back my toilet paper!" I prop myself on my elbows, but the toilet paper is in the wrong pocket and I have to go through a few contortions. She all but presses me to her; my elbows give way. She feels on fire. She's burning hot. "Don't move. Your wound." We lie there. "I've got to go."

"Go, silly."

I scramble down. I kiss her hands.
"I'm going to die," my mother says.
"Ah . . ." I answer.
"I'm afraid, my son."
I can see I've rumpled the sheet badly.

THE LAST THING WE KNOW WHEN WE WRITE A WORK IS HOW IT WILL BEGIN: IN THE NAME OF THE FATHER AND THE SON—

The End.

SOME DAY I'LL WRITE ABOUT ALL THIS IN MORE DETAIL.